The World According to Humphrey

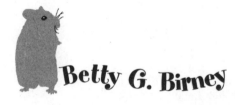

Betty G. Birney

G. P. Putnam's Sons • New York

For more FUN-FUN-FUN
Humphrey adventures look for
Friendship According to Humphrey

To my husband,
Frank
who has been to Brazil, knows all
the state capitals and can
balance a broom on one finger.

Library of Congress Cataloging-in-Publication Data
Birney, Betty G. The world according to Humphrey/Betty G. Birney. p. cm.
Summary: Humphrey, pet hamster at Longfellow School, learns that he has an important role to play in helping his classmates and teacher. [1. Hamsters—Fiction.
2. Schools—Fiction.]
I. Title. PZ7.B5229Wo 2004 [Fic]—dc21 2003005974

ISBN 0-399-24198-1
9 10 8

Contents

The Return of Mrs. Brisbane

Today was the worst day of my life. Ms. Mac left Room 26 of Longfellow School. For good. And that's bad.

Worse yet, Mrs. Brisbane came back. Until today, I didn't even know there was a Mrs. Brisbane. Lucky me.

Now I want to know: What was Ms. Mac thinking? She must have known that soon she'd be leaving without me. And that Mrs. Brisbane would come back to Room 26 and I'd be stuck with her.

I still like—okay, *love*—Ms. Mac more than any human or hamster on earth, but what was she thinking?

"You can learn a lot about yourself by taking care of another species," she told me on the way home the day she got me. "You'll teach those kids a thing or two."

That's what she was thinking. I don't think she was thinking very clearly.

I'm never going to squeak to her again. Of course, I'll probably never see her again because she's GONE-GONE-GONE—but if she comes back, I'm not even going to look at her.

1

(I know that last sentence doesn't make sense. It's hard to make sense when your heart is broken.)

On the other hand, until Ms. Mac arrived, I was going nowhere down at Pet-O-Rama. My days were spent sitting around, looking at a bunch of furry things in cages just like mine. We were treated all right: regular meals, clean cages, music piped in all day.

Over the music, Carl, the store clerk, would answer the phone: "Open nine to nine, seven days a week. Corner of Fifth and Alder, next to the Dairy Maid."

Back then, I feared I'd never see Fifth and Alder, much less the Dairy Maid. Sometimes I'd see human eyes and noses (not always as clean as they should be) poking up against the glass. Nothing ever came of it. The children were excited to see me, but the parents usually had other ideas.

"Oh, come see the fishes, Cornelia. So colorful and so much easier to take care of than a hamster," Mama might say.

Or "No, no, Norbert. They have the cutest little puppies over here. After all, a dog is a boy's best friend."

So there we were: hamsters, gerbils, mice and guinea pigs—not nearly as popular as the fish, cats or dogs. I suspected that I'd be spinning my wheel at Pet-O-Rama forever.

But once Ms. Mac carried me out the door a short six weeks ago, my life changed FAST-FAST-FAST. I saw Fifth! I saw Alder! I saw the Dairy Maid with the statue of a cow in an apron outside!

2

I was dozing when she first came to Pet-O-Rama, as I do during the day because hamsters are more active at night.

"Hello." A warm voice awakened me. When I opened my eyes, I saw a mass of bouncy black curls. A big, happy smile. Huge dark eyes. She smelled of apples. It was love at first sight.

"Aren't you the bright-eyed one?" she asked.

"And might I return the compliment?" I replied. Of course, it came out "Squeak-squeak-squeak," as usual.

Ms. Mac opened up her purse with the big pink and blue flowers on it.

"I'll take him," she told Carl. "He's obviously the most intelligent and handsome hamster you have."

Carl grunted. Then Ms. Mac picked out a respectable cage—okay, not the three-story pagoda I'd had my eye on—but a nice cage.

And soon, amid squeals of encouragement from my friends in the Small Pet Department, from the teeniest white mouse to the lumbering chinchilla, I left Pet-O-Rama with high hopes.

We sped down the street in Ms. Mac's bright yellow car! (She called it a Bug, but I could see it was really a car.) She carried my cage up the stairs to her apartment! We ate apples! We watched TV! She let me run around outside my cage! She gave me my very own name: Humphrey. And she told me all about Room 26, where we'd be going the next morning.

"And since you are an intelligent hamster who is

3

going to school, I have a present for you, Humphrey," she said.

Then she gave me a tiny little notebook and a tiny little pencil. "I got these for you at the doll shop," she explained. She tucked them behind my mirror where no one could see them except me.

"Of course, it might be a while before you learn to read and write," she continued. "But you're smart and I know you'll catch on fast."

Little did she know I could already make out some words from my long, boring days at Pet-O-Rama.

Words like *Chew Toys. Kibble. Pooper-Scoopers.*

Remember, a hamster is grown up at about five weeks old. So if I could learn all the skills I need for life in five weeks, how long could it possibly take to learn to read?

I'll tell you: a week. Yep, in a week I could read and even write a little with the tiny pencil.

In addition to schoolwork, I learned quite a bit about the other students in Room 26. Like Lower-Your-Voice-A.J. and Speak-Up-Sayeh and Wait-for-the-Bell-Garth and Golden-Miranda. (Even after I found out her name is really Miranda Golden, I thought of her as Golden-Miranda because of her long blonde hair. After all, I am a Golden Hamster.)

Yes, life in Room 26 suited me well during the day. My cage had all the comforts a hamster could ask for. I had bars on the window to protect me from my enemies. I had a little sleeping house in one corner where no one could see me or bother me. There was my wheel to spin on, of course, and a lovely pile of nesting material. My mirror came in handy to check my grooming (and to hide my notebook). In one corner, I kept my food. The opposite corner was my bathroom area because hamsters like to keep their poo away from their food. (Who doesn't?) All my needs were taken care of in one convenient cage.

At night, I went home from school with Ms. Mac and we watched TV or listened to music. Sometimes Ms. Mac played her bongo drums. She made a tunnel on the floor so I could race and wiggle to my hamster heart's content.

Oh, the memories of those six weeks with Morgan McNamara. That's her real name, but she told her students to call her Ms. Mac. That's how nice she is. Or was.

On the weekends, Ms. Mac and I had all kinds of adventures. She put me in her shirt pocket (right over her heart!) and took me with her to the laundry room. She had friends over and they laughed and made a fuss over me. She even took me for a bike ride once. I can still feel the wind in my fur!

I didn't have an inkling—until this morning—of the unsqueakable thing she was about to do to me. On the way to work she said, "Humphrey, I hate to tell you, but this is my last day in Room 26 and I'm going to miss you more than you'll ever know."

What was she saying? I hung on to my wheel for dear life!

"You see, it's really Mrs. Brisbane's class. But just before school started, her husband was in an accident, so I took over the class. Today, she's coming back for good."

Good? I could see nothing good in what Ms. Mac was saying.

"Besides, I want to see the world, Humphrey," she told me.

Fine with me. I've thoroughly enjoyed all the world I've seen so far and would go to the ends of the earth with Ms. Mac. But she wasn't finished yet.

"But I can't take you with me."

All hopes dashed. Completely.

"Besides, the kids need you to teach them responsibility. Mrs. Brisbane needs you, too."

∿

Unfortunately, she didn't tell Mrs. Brisbane that.

Mrs. Brisbane was already in Room 26 when we arrived. She smiled at Ms. Mac and shook her hand.

Then she frowned at me and said, "Is that some kind of . . . *rodent*?"

Ms. Mac gave her the speech about how much kids can learn from taking care of another species.

Mrs. Brisbane looked horrified and said, "*I can't stand rodents! Take it back!*"

The *it* she was talking about was *me*.

Ms. Mac didn't bat an eyelash. She put my cage in its usual place next to the window and said the kids were already very attached to me. She attached Dr. Harvey H. Hammer's *Guide to the Care and Feeding of Hamsters* to the cage, along with a chart to make sure I was fed and my cage was cleaned on time.

"The children know what to do. You won't have to do a thing," Ms. Mac said as Mrs. Brisbane glared at me.

Just then, my fellow students came streaming into the room and within half an hour Ms. Mac had said good-bye to everyone, including me.

"I'll never forget you, Humphrey," she whispered. "Don't you forget me, either."

"Not likely. But I don't know if I can ever forgive you," I squeaked.

And then she was gone. Without me.

Mrs. Brisbane didn't even come close to my cage until recess. Then she walked over and said, "Mister, you've got to go."

But she doesn't know my secret: The latch on my cage door doesn't work. It never has. It's the lock-that-doesn't-lock.

So I've got news for Mrs. Brisbane: If I've got to go, it will be when and where *I* decide to go. Not her.

Meanwhile, I'm not turning my back on this woman. Not for a second. If I ever disappear and someone finds this notebook, just check out Mrs. Brisbane. Please!

TIP ONE: Choose your new hamster's home very carefully and make sure it is secure. Hamsters are skillful "escape artists" and once out of their cages they are *very* difficult to find.

Guide to the Care and Feeding of Hamsters, Dr. Harvey H. Hammer

Night Life

For the rest of the day, I felt SAD-SAD-SAD.

"You look sad, Humphrey," Golden-Miranda said when she was cleaning my cage right before lunch.

According to the chart Ms. Mac had left, it was her turn to take care of me, thank goodness. Miranda was the best cage-cleaner and never said "Yuck!"

She put on throwaway gloves, then cleaned my potty corner, changed my bedding, gave me fresh water and finally—oh, joy!—gave me fresh grain, some lettuce and mealworms.

"This will make you happy," she said as she slipped me the special treat she'd brought from home: cauliflower. Naturally, Miranda had good taste. I promptly saved it in my cheek pouch until I could store it in my sleeping house. Hamsters like to stash food for the future.

After my cage was taken care of, I felt well enough to observe Mrs. Brisbane more carefully.

Now, Ms. Mac was tall, wore bright blouses, short skirts and high shoes. She wore bracelets that jingled-jangled. She spoke in a loud voice and waved her arms and walked all around the room when she taught.

Mrs. Brisbane, on the other hand, was short with short gray hair. She wore dark clothes and flat shoes and she didn't jingle-jangle at all. She spoke in a voice just loud enough to hear and sat at her desk or stood at the chalkboard when she taught.

No wonder I was feeling drowsy after lunch. All that nice food and all that soft talking.

"Is that all this hamster does—sleep?" she asked at one point when she glanced over at my cage.

"Well, he's 'turnal," replied Raise-Your-Hand-Heidi Hopper.

"Raise-Your-Hand-Heidi," said Mrs. Brisbane. "What's 'turnal?"

"You know. 'Turnal. He sleeps during the day," said Heidi.

I was wide-awake now. "Nocturnal," I squeaked. "Hamsters are *nocturnal*."

"Oh, you mean *nocturnal*," said Mrs. Brisbane, almost as if she had understood me. She turned and wrote the word on the board. "Can anyone else name an animal that's nocturnal?"

"Owl," said Heidi.

"Raise-Your-Hand-Heidi," said Mrs. Brisbane. "But that is correct. An owl is nocturnal. Anyone else?"

A voice shouted out, "My dad!"

Mrs. Brisbane looked around. "Who said that?"

"He did. A.J." Garth Tugwell pointed at A.J.

9

Both boys sat at the table nearest to my cage.

"What about your dad?" Mrs. Brisbane asked.

A.J. squirmed in his seat. "Well, my mom always says my dad is nocturnal 'cause he stays up so late watching TV."

Stop-Giggling-Gail and a few other students snickered. Mrs. Brisbane didn't crack a smile.

"Her use of the word is correct," she said. "Though, technically, humans are not nocturnal. Any others?"

Eventually, the class came up with more names of nocturnal animals, like bats and coyotes and opossums, and Mrs. Brisbane said that the class would be learning more about animal habits later in the year.

If she'd just look at me, she could learn a lot. But I noticed for the rest of the day that Mrs. Brisbane stayed far away from my cage, as if I had a disease or something.

She read a mighty fine story to us in the afternoon, though. In fact, I couldn't get back to my nap afterward. It was about a scary house and these scratching noises and . . . a ghost! THUMP-THUMP-THUMP, the ghost came down the hall! Oh, I had shivers and quivers.

I have to say, Mrs. Brisbane knows how to read a story. Her voice changed and her eyes got wide and I forgot about her gray hair and her dark suit. To squeak the truth, my fur was on end! The story had a funny ending because it turned out the ghost wasn't a ghost at all. It was an owl!

At the end of the story, everybody laughed. Even Mrs. Brisbane.

I was beginning to think that life with this new teacher wouldn't be so bad. But I changed my mind when the bell rang at the end of the day and all my classmates raced out of the room, leaving me alone with *her.*

She erased the chalkboard and gathered up her papers. I could tell that we'd be going home soon. Suddenly, I began to worry. What if Mrs. Brisbane lived in a scary house with spooky noises and a thumping ghost?

Or, even worse, what if Mrs. Brisbane had a scary pet, like a dog?

My mind was racing as fast as I was spinning my wheel when she finally approached and looked down at me, frowning.

"Well, you're on your own now," she said.

With that, she closed the blinds and walked away. But I heard her mutter "rodent" under her breath.

She left the classroom and closed the door.

She left me alone. All alone in Room 26.

I had never ever been alone before.

As the room slowly grew darker and quieter, I thought back to the happy times at Ms. Mac's apartment. There were always cheery lights on and music and telephone-talking and . . . oh, dear, during the day I never noticed how the clock on the wall ticked off the seconds one by one very loudly.

TICK-TICK-TICK. I was feeling SICK-SICK-SICK.

I wondered if there were any owls around Room 26. Or ghosts.

I tried to pass the time by writing in my notebook about Pet-O-Rama and my days at Ms. Mac's apartment. Writing took my mind off my jittery nerves. But eventually, my writing paw began to ache and I had to stop my scratchings. If only I could roam free, as I had at Ms. Mac's apartment!

Then I remembered the lock-that-doesn't-lock.

It only took a few seconds to jiggle the door open. I skittered across the table. Then, grasping the top of the table leg tightly, I closed my eyes and slid to the ground.

Ah, freedom! I dashed along the shiny floor. I darted between the tables and chairs. I stopped to nibble a peanut underneath Stop-Giggling-Gail's chair. It tasted delicious and made the coolest crunching sound. I chewed and chomped and gnawed and nibbled. And when I stopped . . . I heard the sound.

THUMP-THUMP-THUMP.

Just like the story Mrs. Brisbane had read us.

THUMP-THUMP-THUMP.

Closer and closer down the hall, coming toward Room 26.

Then RATTLE-SCRATCH. RATTLE-SCRATCH. THUMP-THUMP-THUMP.

Suddenly, I longed for the protective comfort of my cage. I dropped what was left of the peanut and scampered back. But when I got to the table, I thought a terrible thought. I had slid down the smooth, shiny leg, straight down. But how was I going to climb up again?

I flung myself against the table leg, grabbed on and pushed UP-UP-UP. But I had only made a little progress when I began to slide DOWN-DOWN-DOWN. I was right back where I'd started.

The rattling got louder. The sounds weren't coming toward Room 26 anymore. They were coming *in* Room 26.

Just then, I noticed a long cord running down from the blinds. Without hesitation, I leaped up and grabbed the cord and began swinging back and forth. My stomach churned and I wished I'd never touched that peanut. But with each swing, I got a little higher off the ground. As soon as I saw the edge of the table, I closed my eyes and dived toward it.

Whoosh! I slid across the table and scampered into the cage. As I pulled the door behind me, I was suddenly blinded by light.

The something had turned on the lights and was clomping across the floor. It was huge and heavy and coming right toward me.

Just then, my eyes adjusted to the light and I saw the thing. It was a man!

"Well, well, who have we here? A new student!" a voice boomed.

The man was smiling down at me. My, that was a lovely piece of fur across his upper lip. A nice black mustache. He bent down to peer in at me.

"I'm Aldo Amato. And who are you?"

"I'm Humphrey . . . and you scared me half to death!" I told him. But as always, all that came out was "Squeak-squeak-squeak."

Aldo squinted at the sign on my cage.

13

"Oh, you're Humphrey! Hope I didn't scare you half to death!" he said with a laugh.

"I've just come to clean the room. I come every night. But where have you been?" he said. He rolled up a big cart with a bucket and mops and brooms and all kinds of bottles and rags on it.

"Oh, that's right," he replied as if we were having a real conversation. "Mrs. Brisbane came back today. She's a good teacher, you know, Humphrey. Been teaching here a long time. Wish I'd had a good teacher like her. Say . . . do you like music, Humphrey?"

"SQUEAK-SQUEAK-SQUEAK." I tried to tell him I love music almost as much as I love Ms. Mac. Suddenly, a song came blasting out of the radio on his cart and he set to work: sweeping, mopping, moving desks, dusting.

But Aldo Amato didn't just dust and mop. He spun and swayed. He hopped and leaped. He twisted and twirled.

"How do you like the floor show?" Aldo asked me as he grasped the mop like a dancer holding his partner. "Get it? It's a floor show! 'Cause I'm cleaning the floor!"

Then Aldo roared the biggest roar of a laugh I'd ever heard. His big mustache shook so much, I thought it might fall off.

"You like that? I'll show you real talent, Humphrey!" Aldo Amato picked up his broom and very carefully stood it up with the very tip balancing on one out-stretched fingertip. It wiggled from side to side, but Aldo moved with the broom and managed to keep it balanced

14

straight in the air for an amazingly long time. When he was finished, he bowed deeply and said, "What do you think? I'm going to join the circus!" And he roared again.

Then Aldo wiped his forehead with a big bandanna and sat down at the table where A.J. usually sits. "You know what, Humphrey? You're such good company, I think I'll take my dinner break with you. Do you mind?"

"PLEASE-PLEASE-PLEASE," I squeaked.

Aldo pulled his chair right up to my cage.

"Hey, you're a handsome guy . . . like me. Here . . . a little bit of green won't hurt you, will it?" He tore off a piece of lettuce from his sandwich and pushed it through the bars. Of course, I hid it in my cheek pouch.

Aldo chuckled. "Good for you, Humphrey! Always save something for a rainy day."

The two of us shared a very pleasant meal as Aldo told me about how he used to a have a regular job where he worked during the day. But then, his company closed down and he couldn't find a job for a long time. He couldn't even pay the rent when he was lucky enough to get hired here at Longfellow School. He was glad to get the job, but it's lonely working at night because his friends work during the day. They can never get together like they used to.

I tried to squeak to him about all the creatures, like me, that are also nocturnal and Aldo listened.

"I know you're trying to tell me something, Humphrey, but I can't tell what it is. Maybe you're just saying I'm not alone after all, huh?"

"Squeak." He understood!

Aldo stood up and threw his trash into the plastic bag on his cart.

"Well, I've got a lot of other rooms to clean, my friend. But I'll be back tomorrow night. Maybe I'll take my dinner break with you again."

Aldo pushed his cart toward the door and reached for the light switch.

"NO-NO-NO!" I squeaked, dreading the thought of being plunged into darkness again.

Aldo stopped. "I hate to leave you in the dark. But if I don't turn off the lights, I could lose my job."

He clomped back across the floor to the window. "Tell you what. I'll leave the blinds open a little. There's a nice light right outside your window."

After he turned off the lights and left, I chomped on the lettuce I'd saved and basked in the warm glow of the streetlight—and my new friendship with Aldo.

TIP TWO: Hamsters are not picky about their food and eat very little. Make sure to feed your pet a wide variety of tasty foods.

Guide to the Care and Feeding of Hamsters, Dr. Harvey H. Hammer

The Two Faces of Mrs. Brisbane

That week was BUSY-BUSY-BUSY, but I learned a lot. I learned all the capitals of the United States. (I didn't say I remembered them all, but I learned them all.)

I learned about how water changes from solid to liquid to gas.

I learned how to subtract fractions.

I learned something else. Something very weird. There are two Mrs. Brisbanes.

And I thought one Mrs. Brisbane was one too many.

The first Mrs. Brisbane is a good teacher, just like Aldo said. She's better than Ms. Mac was at getting A.J. to lower his voice. She's better at getting Heidi to raise her hand before she blurts something out loud.

Of course, nobody could get Speak-Up-Sayeh to raise her hand or to blurt anything out loud. Sayeh is so quiet and gentle, she never gives an answer. If the teacher calls on her, she stares down at her desk without saying a word.

But when it's Sayeh's turn to clean my cage and feed

me, she holds me in her hand so gently, I feel like I'm floating on a cloud. "Hello, Humphrey," she whispers. "Your fur is so beautiful." I always feel calmer when Sayeh holds me.

She's so nice, I wish Mrs. Brisbane would leave her alone. Ms. Mac hardly ever called on Sayeh once she realized how shy she was. But Mrs. Brisbane calls on her all the time. She won't leave her alone.

"Sayeh, speak up, please. I know you know the answer," she'd say while Sayeh stared at the top of her desk as if she were watching a TV show there. But I was shocked when Mrs. Brisbane got annoyed with Sayeh—sweet, shy Sayeh—and said, "You will stay in during recess."

Sayeh still stared down without moving a muscle. But a minute later, I saw something wet drop from Sayeh's eye to the tabletop.

I hated Mrs. Brisbane.

Of course, I don't go out to recess. In fact, I'm glad, since it's a great time to catch up on my sleep. So I was there when Mrs. Brisbane talked to Sayeh. And I was all ready to squeak up on her behalf, if necessary.

Mrs. Brisbane brought a stack of papers to the table and sat down across from Sayeh.

"Sayeh, you think I'm being mean to you, don't you?"

Sayeh slowly shook her head no. I heartily nodded my head yes, but no one was looking at me.

"But I wouldn't call on you if I didn't know that you know the answers," the teacher explained. "Look at your papers and tests. You get 100% on everything: spelling, science, geography and arithmetic. Your vocabulary is excellent. But I have never heard you speak. Can you tell me why?"

I checked my notebook and I was pretty impressed. I only got an 85% on the last vocabulary test. This girl is smart!

Sayeh still did not speak.

"Sayeh, I'm going to have to send a note home to your parents. Maybe they can help me figure out what to do," said Mrs. Brisbane.

Sayeh looked up, very frightened. "No, please," she said.

Mrs. Brisbane looked surprised. She reached over and patted Sayeh's arm. "I won't send a note now . . . if you'll promise to try."

Sayeh looked back down at the desk and nodded.

"I'll tell you what. I won't call on you if you promise that sometime within the next week you'll raise your hand on your own and answer a question. Is that a deal?"

Sayeh nodded, very slowly this time.

"You have to say it," Mrs. Brisbane told her.

"Deal," Sayeh whispered.

"Terrific!" said Mrs. Brisbane, smiling. "Now, how would you like to erase the board for me?"

Sayeh jumped up and hurried to the board. All the students in Room 26 like to erase the board for some reason.

Mrs. Brisbane was sure hard to figure out. She hadn't

been mean to Sayeh at all. She just did what a teacher is supposed to do.

I liked this Mrs. Brisbane. I even liked the pink blouse she had on.

But at the end of the day when the students were gone, the second Mrs. Brisbane came back.

The really scary one.

She straightened up the room and came over to the window to close the blinds. I could only hope that Aldo would open them for me later.

She looked down and saw that the table around me was messy. The bag of shavings used for my bedding had torn and bits of litter were scattered all over the table. Garth had done the cleaning and left the lid off my treats box. The whole table looked untidy.

"Good grief," said Mrs. Brisbane in a very unhappy voice.

I decided to take a spin on my wheel. Usually, that cheers people up. But not Mrs. Brisbane.

She started to clean the table, getting paper towels and cleaning spray and muttering to herself the whole time.

"Not my job," she grumbled. "These children are not responsible. All I need is somebody else to take care of. Some . . . rodent!"

Nobody says *rodent* quite the way Mrs. Brisbane does.

Then she looked down at me with angry eyes and said, "You . . . are . . . a . . . trouble . . . maker. And somehow, I'm going to get rid of you!"

Then she grabbed her purse and her papers and stormed out of Room 26.

For once, I didn't mind being left alone. I didn't even mind the TICK-TICK-TICK of the clock.

I was just GLAD-GLAD-GLAD that the second Mrs. Brisbane was gone.

I was worried about what she'd said, but I kept my mind occupied by practicing my vocabulary words until the light was completely gone. (If Sayeh got 100% correct, why couldn't I?)

Then I sat and waited.

Suddenly, bright lights blinded my eyes as the door swung open and a familiar voice roared, "Never fear— Aldo's here!"

Aldo rolled his cart over to my cage and put his face right down next to mine.

"How's it going, Humphrey?" he asked.

I tried squeaking out my story, but Aldo didn't quite catch what I was saying.

"Whoa, pal! Something's got your tail in a tizzy! Well, this should cheer you up!" Aldo reached into a brown paper bag, pulled something out and dangled it in front of my cage.

"Something to gnaw on, little buddy," he said, opening the door.

JOY-JOY-JOY! A tiny dog biscuit! One of Ms. Mac's friends gave me one of these once. You can crunch on it forever.

"Ha-ha! Suddenly, there's a smile on your face!" Aldo

21

beamed with pride. "Now I'll clean this room real fast so we can eat our dinner together."

꧁ ꧂

I never saw anybody move as fast as Aldo. He turned the music up full blast. Then he mopped and polished and swept and scrubbed, while I nibbled and gnawed on my biscuit.

When he was finished, Aldo pulled a chair up to my cage and took out his big sandwich.

"You know, Humphrey, some folks might think I'm crazy, talking to a hamster. But you're better company than a lot of people I know. Here . . . have a nice salad. It's good for you!"

He tore off a tiny piece of lettuce and pushed it through the wires of my cage.

"Thank you," I squeaked.

"You're welcome," said Aldo.

"So, what were we talking about last night? Oh, yeah. Loneliness. You know, I have friends, Humphrey. But during the day, when I'd like to do something—go bowling or to a movie or something—they're at work. And when they want to do something, I'm at work. Of course there's the weekend, but I usually see my family, you know. My brother and his family, my nieces and nephews—I got a big family."

Suddenly Aldo bopped the side of his head with the palm of his hand. "Whoa, Humphrey. I never told you. My nephew . . . he's in your class. Richie Rinaldi. He sits over there."

He pointed to the far side of the room. "He always has the neatest desk in the class. He'd better or he'll hear from his uncle. Do you know him?"

"Of course," I squeaked. Repeat-That-Please-Richie. One of the nicest boys in the class. But he mumbled a lot and usually had to repeat something two or three times to be understood.

Aldo crunched his bag and tossed it into his trash can. "Well, I'm out of here. You know, they got a frog in Room 16, but he's not good company like you are. He sings nice, though."

Sing! I'll sing for you, Aldo, I thought. "SQUEAK-SQUEAK-SQUEAK!"

"Don't worry. I don't like him nearly as much as you, my friend," Aldo said. He opened the blinds to let the light in.

Just as he was going out the door, Aldo said, "See you next week, Humphrey!"

Next week! A cold chill came over me. Tomorrow was Friday. When Ms. Mac was in Room 26, she took me home for the weekend. But if Mrs. Brisbane didn't take me home, I'd have two very long days and nights with no one—not even Aldo—to feed me or chat with me.

Even worse, what if Mrs. Brisbane did take me to her house? What fate would await me there?

I had plenty to keep me busy the rest of the night: worrying about Mrs. Brisbane and how she planned to do away with me. Ms. Mac . . . please come back!

TIP THREE: Hamsters enjoy a change in routine. Among their favorite activities are eating, grooming themselves, climbing, running, spinning, taking a nap and being petted.

Guide to the Care and Feeding of Hamsters, Dr. Harvey H. Hammer

The Most Important Man in the World

Luckily, Friday went by smoothly. Sorry to say, Sayeh didn't raise her hand. But Heidi Hopper did—amazing! A.J. actually whispered. Richie cleaned my cage. I tried to imagine him with a big black mustache like his uncle Aldo.

Later, when Mrs. Brisbane asked him to name the capital of Kentucky, Richie said, "Hot dog."

Everyone giggled, of course. Especially Stop-Giggling-Gail. Otherwise known as Gail Morgenstern.

"Repeat-That-Please-Richie," said the teacher.

Richie realized he'd made a mistake, so he tried again. "Frankfurter," he said.

More giggles. Explosive giggles.

"Try again, Richie," said Mrs. Brisbane, who was on the verge of smiling herself.

"Uh . . . Frankfort!" he said proudly.

(That was the correct answer, by the way.)

So, you see, it wasn't exactly a bad day in Room 26. It's just that I was jittery, wondering what would happen to me when the bell rang. Would I be left alone . . . hungry, utterly forsaken for two whole days? Or would I be a captive in the haunted house of Mrs. Brisbane?

At last, the bell rang and the students flew out of the door like a flock of homing pigeons in a movie Ms. Mac showed us.

Just then, the room mothers stopped by. One was Heidi Hopper's mom and the other one was Art Patel's. (That's Pay-Attention-Art.) They came to talk to Mrs. Brisbane about Halloween, which was less than two weeks away.

I didn't know what Halloween was, but it sure sounded scary, especially when they talked about bringing bats and witches and even worse—cats—right into the classroom! SHIVER-QUIVER-SHAKE. What could they be thinking?

I was about ready to fling open the door of my cage and escape when the door opened and in walked the principal, Mr. Morales.

Mr. Morales is the Most Important Person at Longfellow School. He runs the place and everyone respects him. You can tell. For one thing, Mr. Morales always wears a tie. No one else in the whole school wears a tie except Mr. Morales. For another thing, when Mr. Morales comes into the room, everyone stops what they're doing and waits to see what he has to say. And for a third thing, both Ms. Mac and Mrs. Brisbane sometimes threatened to send a misbehaving student to Mr. Morales's office. As soon as the teacher mentioned the principal's name, the student would start acting very, very nice.

"Good afternoon, ladies," said Mr. Morales. He was wearing a light blue shirt and a tie that had tiny books all over it.

Everyone said, "Hello."

"Well, how's your first week back, Sue?" he asked.

"Sue" was apparently Mrs. Brisbane, although I'd never actually thought of her having a first name before.

She said it was great to be back and what a wonderful class it was, which obviously pleased the room mothers.

Then Mr. Morales leaned over my cage and smiled. His tie dangled right over my head.

"I'll bet you're enjoying this furry little pupil," he said with a grin.

I expected Mrs. Brisbane to tell him what a trouble-making rodent I was. But instead, she forced a smile and said, "Well, yes, but he's quite a bit of extra work."

Mr. Morales waved a finger at me. He didn't seem to hear what Mrs. Brisbane said.

"I always wanted one of these fellows," he said. "But my papa wouldn't let me have one. Sure is cute."

Mrs. Brisbane cleared her throat. "Yes, but I'm afraid he's a little distracting. I was going to see if Mr. Kim in Room 12 wants him."

I was shocked. Luckily, so were the room mothers.

"Oh, no! The children just love Humphrey," said Mrs. Patel.

"Heidi talks about him all the time. And it's a wonderful way to teach the kids responsibility," Mrs. Hopper said.

"Yes, but it's a little too much responsibility for me." Mrs. Brisbane sighed. "At least I have a couple days away from him this weekend."

"You're not taking him home with you?" asked Mrs. Patel.

Mrs. Brisbane backed away from the cage. "Oh, no. It's out of the question."

"But Ms. Mac always took him home," said Mrs. Hopper.

"He'll be fine. He has plenty of food," Mrs. Brisbane answered very, very firmly.

The room mothers were silent a second. Mr. Morales was still wiggling his finger at me.

Then Mrs. Hopper spoke up. "Why don't the kids take turns bringing Humphrey home for the weekend? They can sign up, we'll talk to their parents and give them instructions. It will be a great experience!"

"Some people might not want him," said Mrs. Brisbane.

Squeak for yourself, Mrs. Brisbane!

"That's fine," said Mrs. Hopper. "There'll be plenty who will."

"I think it's great," Mrs. Patel agreed. "I'd take him today, but we're going up to the lake for the weekend."

"Oh, I'd take him, too," said Mrs. Hopper. "But we're painting the house and the place is a mess. Next week for sure."

"Yes, I could do it next week," Mrs. Patel agreed.

Mrs. Brisbane smiled a fake smile. "So who's going to take him this weekend?"

The room mothers looked at one another.

"I could make a few quick calls. Maybe the Rinaldis," Mrs. Patel suggested.

"CALL-CALL-CALL," I squeaked.

Suddenly, Mr. Morales stood up straight. "I have a better idea," he announced. "I'll take Humphrey home for the weekend. My kids will love him. Then, starting next week, you can have the students take turns."

The three women were almost as surprised as I was.

"Don't worry. He'll be in good hands," Mr. Morales assured them.

Well, I guess I would be. After all, I was going home with the Most Important Person at Longfellow School!

As he drove me to his house, Mr. Morales told me how he'd always wanted a hamster when he was a kid. But his dad always said they didn't need another mouth to feed. "I argued with him, Humphrey. I said, 'Papa, I will feed him off my own plate.' Then Papa said we'd have to buy the cage and stuff to put in it. I guess he was right, Humphrey. We couldn't afford it."

He smiled his big smile. "But not anymore. Now I'm the principal of my own school."

I told you he was important.

His house was nice, but I didn't get to see much of it because as soon as we came in the door, two little whirl-winds tumbled into the room, shrieking and squealing.

"Quiet down, now. You'll frighten the little fellow," Mr. Morales told them. He got that right.

He introduced us. The little boy, who was about five, was named Willy. He kept poking his fingers through the wires of the cage. I was about to bite him— pure instinct—but then I remembered: This is the son of the Most Important Person at Longfellow School. So I didn't.

The little girl, who was about seven, was named Brenda. She kept sticking her face up against the cage and squealing. I tried squeaking back at her, but I don't think she could hear me.

Mr. Morales tried to quiet them down. He explained that I was a guest for the weekend and they had to treat me with respect.

They didn't listen.

A pretty lady rushed through the room, jingling her car keys. "I'm late. I have a house to show." She glanced in my direction. "We'll talk about *that* later. *Adiós.*"

Mr. Morales wished her luck and she was gone. Then he carried me into the den with Willy and Brenda clinging to his legs and yelping.

My cage was swinging back and forth so much, I was getting airsick. Or cage-sick.

Mr. Morales set my cage on a table in their family room.

"Now get back and listen to me," he told his children. "I'll tell you all about him."

"Can we take him out?" screamed Willy.

"Can we put him in my room?" shouted Brenda. "Can he sleep with me tonight?"

"We can't do anything until you settle down," Mr. Morales said.

Bravo, Mr. Morales, I thought.

But still, the children didn't listen. The Most Important Person at Longfellow School was not treated with respect in his own house.

Willy lurched forward and swung open the cage door.

"Oooh, there's *poo* in there!" he screamed.

"Where? Where?" shrieked Brenda.

Willy pointed to my potty corner, which I thought was unsqueakably rude of him.

"I want to hold him," said Brenda, grabbing me.

She squeezed me so hard, I let out a squeal.

"Stop!" said Mr. Morales. "Put him back right now!"

She opened her hand and dropped me onto the floor of my cage. Luckily, I landed in a pile of soft bedding.

Luckily, I didn't land in my poo.

I was a little dizzy, but I heard Mr. Morales send Willy and Brenda to their rooms.

"I will not allow you to mistreat an animal. Upstairs. Doors shut. No playing until I say you can," he said.

Suddenly, Mr. Morales didn't look so important. He slumped down in the chair next to my cage and loosened his tie.

"Now you know my secret, Humphrey. At school, everybody listens to me. At home, nobody listens to me," he said.

Mr. Morales looked TIRED-TIRED-TIRED.

Above our heads came the sounds of thumping and bumping. It sounded as if the ceiling was about to fall in.

"They're bouncing on their beds, Humphrey. Not supposed to do that, either," he said.

He slowly rose and went to the stairway in the hall.

"Willy! Brenda! Stop that now!" he yelled.

Surprisingly, the thumping and bumping stopped.

"They listened!" I squeaked when the principal sat down again. But the thumping and bumping began again in a minute.

"I wish I knew what to do," he said. "Some way to teach them a lesson."

I nodded. A lesson is just what those children needed.

And I was just the hamster to teach them.

TIP FOUR: Never, ever squeeze, pinch or crush a hamster. If it runs away, squeals or mutters, leave the hamster alone.

Guide to the Care and Feeding of Hamsters, Dr. Harvey H. Hammer

Plans Are Hatched

When Mr. Morales went into the kitchen to get a glass of water, I carefully opened the lock-that-doesn't-lock and slipped out of my cage. I leaped over to the chair, then scampered down to the floor and hid in the corner, behind the long curtains.

Mr. Morales returned and sat down again. The children were still thumping and bumping and were now screaming and screeching as well.

"Say, Humphrey, maybe you need some water, too," he said and leaned toward my cage.

Mr. Morales gasped when he saw that it was empty. "Humphrey, where did you go? Oh, I should have known you'd escape! I'd run away from those kids if I could, too. But do me a favor, Humphrey. *Please come out!*"

In a panic, he darted around the room. "The kids in Room 26 will hate me if I lose you!" he said.

I felt sorry for Mr. Morales, so I scratched around a little.

"There you are!" he said, bending down to look at me. "Now, let's get you back in your cage."

Not quite yet, I thought. He reached down to pick me up and I scampered forward, just a few inches past his hand.

"Don't do this to me, Humphrey," he said. "Cooperate."

But I wasn't doing anything *to* him. I was doing something *for* him.

"Work with me," he said, but this time to himself. "Maybe . . . hey, that's it!" He looked down at me. "With your help, Humphrey."

Mr. Morales really swung into action then.

He raced upstairs. The thumping and bumping stopped. When he raced back downstairs, Willy and Brenda were with him.

"Close all the doors, Willy," he said.

"But, Dad," Willy whined.

"Close them," his father repeated firmly. "Now!"

Willy closed all the doors.

"You two scared poor Humphrey with your screaming and poking and thumping. We may never see him again!" he told them.

Brenda burst into tears. "Humphrey's dead!" she sobbed.

"No. Humphrey's too smart for that," Mr. Morales told her. "But he will run away if you two aren't nice to him."

RIGHT-RIGHT-RIGHT. You have to be pretty smart to be a principal.

"Now, do you want to help me get Humphrey back?"

"YES!" the children shouted.

Mr. Morales explained the Plan. He said the only way they'd get me back in my cage was if they worked together. And they could only work together if they listened to him. Really listened.

They were listening now. And they kept listening, too. Because he told them the most important thing they could do was to be quiet.

So they were quiet.

"I'm pretty sure he's still in the room. Our job is to lure him back into his cage," Mr. Morales whispered.

He put my cage in the middle of the floor. Then he went to the kitchen and got a handful of sunflower seeds. Willy and Brenda helped him make a trail of seeds across the floor leading up to the cage.

"Good," said Mr. Morales. "Now we have to be very, very quiet and wait for Humphrey to pick up the seeds. But if you say anything or even move, you might scare him."

"We'll be quiet, Dad," said Willy. Brenda agreed.

They all sat on the sofa.

"Do you think it will work?" Willy whispered.

"Of course," Brenda answered. "Dad's smart."

Well, he's not the only one.

I waited for a while. After all, the Morales children needed all the practice staying quiet they could get. When Willy got restless, I started skittering along the floor.

"I hear him!" said Brenda.

"Shhh," said Willy.

I waited a few more seconds, then scrambled out of

the corner and grabbed the closest seed. I could hear loud gasps from the children, but I pretended not to notice.

I scurried toward the second seed. This Plan Mr. Morales and I came up with was TASTY-TASTY-TASTY.

I could almost feel three pairs of eyes fixed on me, but I ignored them. I grabbed up the third and fourth seeds, hid them in my cheek pouch, then stopped right outside the open door of my cage.

Inside, Mr. Morales had left a lovely pile of sunflower seeds.

It was nice to be free, but my cage was home after all.

Besides, until the day somebody fixes the lock-that-doesn't-lock, I can get out whenever I want.

The kids were still quiet, so I made a run for the cage. Mr. Morales quickly closed the door and the children began to cheer.

"We did it!" said Brenda.

"Dad's the smartest man in the world!" said Willy.

"Hey, you kids helped. When we cooperate and work together, we make a pretty good team," Mr. Morales told them.

"*¡Lo mejor!*" Willy agreed. "The best!"

Mr. Morales squatted down and winked at me. "Of course, Humphrey helped, too."

I'll say.

The rest of the weekend with the Morales family was fine. Sometimes the kids started interrupting their dad or mom, but Mr. Morales just reminded them that they could be polite if they tried.

Willy and Brenda tried.

Mrs. Morales sold a house (it turns out that selling other people's houses is her job), so they celebrated with pizza and ice cream.

Brenda learned to hold me gently.

Willy even cleaned the poo out of my cage, which I appreciated.

Life is good, I thought as Mr. Morales drove me back to school Monday morning.

Then I remembered Mrs. Brisbane. And how she'd said I was a troublemaker and she was going to get rid of me.

"Humphrey, you are a true friend," said Mr. Morales as he carried my cage back into Room 26. "I'll never forget what you did for me."

As soon as class started on Monday, Heidi's mom came into the classroom and explained to everyone about taking me home on weekends.

"How many of you would be interested?" Mrs. Hopper asked.

Every single hand in the classroom was raised.

Every hand except one: Mrs. Brisbane's.

Still, it was a pretty good week.

I got a 90% on the vocabulary test. I'll bet Sayeh got 100%. But she still didn't raise her hand, even though she'd promised.

And Aldo talked more and more every night. On Tuesday night, he leaned in close and asked, "Humphrey, don't you ever wish you had a girlfriend?"

Like most hamsters, I'm pretty much of a loner, so I really hadn't thought about it before.

"Not sure," I squeaked.

"I would like one," said Aldo. "A real nice girlfriend."

I felt so sorry for Aldo, I squeaked extra loud when he performed his broom-balancing act for me.

I was still thinking about him on Wednesday. After everyone had left, while there was still light coming in the window, I meandered outside the cage to help myself to any mealworms that Heidi might have left behind when she fed me earlier in the day.

The table was covered with newspapers and while I nibbled, I browsed the news. All of life was there on the pages of the newspaper. Births and deaths. Lost pets (SAD-SAD-SAD). Funny jokes. Good news and bad news.

Then there were the ads. My, there were so many stores. Not just Pet-O-Rama but Shoes-O-Rama and Food-O-Rama and Books Galore and Wide World of Tools!

And there were other ads, too. One in particular caught my eye that afternoon. It read:

**WORK NIGHTS? LONELY? WANT TO MEET
OTHERS WHO WORK NIGHTS?**

THE MOONLIGHTERS CLUB

**FOR PEOPLE WHO WORK AT NIGHT.
MEETINGS ARE HELD DURING THE DAY ON WEEKDAYS.
HIKES AND OUTINGS TO RESTAURANTS, PARKS, PLAYS,
MOVIES AND MUCH MORE!**

There was a name and a phone number at the end.

I could hardly believe it. This was exactly what Aldo needed! I could already see him, smiling and happy, going to parks and plays with the Moonlighters Club and having a girlfriend.

But how could I get Aldo to read this ad? He'd probably just throw it away. Still, if I cut it out and left it in a place where he couldn't miss it, well, maybe.

Hamsters can't do scissors, but we have nifty teeth. It took me a while to nibble the whole ad out neatly, but I did a pretty good job. Then I stood the clipping up against my cage. Aldo couldn't help but see it if he looked at me, which he always did.

That evening, I was more anxious than usual for Aldo to arrive. When he turned on the lights, I squeaked, "Hello," right away.

"Greetings to you, my little friend," said Aldo as he pushed his cart into the room. "You sound like you have something on your mind."

"You bet," I tried to tell him.

He ambled over to my cage and leaned down to look in.

"What's happening, Humphrey?" he asked.

I saw his eyes light on the scrap of newspaper.

"Hey, I can hardly see you." He reached out and pushed the clipping aside.

"Read it!" I squeaked right out. Of course, he didn't understand.

He didn't even look at what the ad said. He just set it down next to the cage and leaned in closer.

I was squeaking a blue streak. "Look at it now!"

"Calm down, Humphrey. I've got a treat for you," said Aldo. He reached into his pocket and pulled out a tiny bit of carrot. "Your pal Aldo would never forget you."

My heart sank. You try to help a human and they don't even pay attention. But as you know, I don't give up easily.

I squeaked happily while he balanced his broom on one finger, as usual. But my mind was on the Moon-lighters Club and how to get Aldo there.

After he left, I scrambled out of my cage, picked up the newspaper clipping and tucked it inside my note-book. Then I hid the notebook behind my mirror. If I didn't, somebody mean (like Mrs. Brisbane) might throw it away.

I was still wondering what to do with it the next day when Mrs. Brisbane rolled in a cart with a big machine on it.

"This is the overhead projector," she told the class. "I'm going to use it for some map work."

When Mrs. Brisbane turned the machine on, a bright light was projected onto the wall. Then she placed a paper map on the glass and suddenly that map showed up really big on the wall. She could write on it and draw on it and you could see everything she wrote.

A machine like this could come in very handy, I thought.

So when Mrs. Brisbane turned the machine off and

sent my classmates off to lunch, I thought about that machine.

When A.J. cleaned my cage and changed my water and bedding, I thought about that machine.

I thought about it so hard, I suddenly came up with a REALLY-REALLY-REALLY good Plan. But it would be difficult to carry out and dangerous as well.

TIP FIVE: If a hamster manages to escape his cage, you can sometimes lure him back in with a trail of sunflower seeds.

Guide to the Care and Feeding of Hamsters, Dr. Harvey H. Hammer

Moonlight Madness

I waited until the school was completely quiet. No students, no teachers, no Mr. Morales.

Then I got busy because I had a lot of work to do. Big work for a small hamster.

First, I took the Moonlighters Club clipping out of my notebook. Holding it in my mouth, I opened the lock-that-doesn't-lock and scurried across the table.

Getting down off that table was still a problem. I grabbed hold of the leg and slid down, as I've done before. It makes me feel a little queasy in my tummy. But it would be worthwhile if I could get Aldo a girlfriend.

I hurried over to the big machine, which was very, very high off the ground. It seemed impossible for me to get up there, but I had it all planned out in my mind. Crawl up the wastebasket—oooh, I didn't know it would sway like that! Leap over to the seat of Mrs. Brisbane's chair. Whoa—slippery! Crawl up the rungs to the chalkboard tray behind it. Along the chalkboard tray to the bookcase. Then the hardest part: the dive from the bookcase to the overhead projector cart. If you ever try it yourself, don't look down!

I was practically home free, but I still had to get up to the lit part. Still holding the newspaper clipping in my mouth, I grabbed on to a big screw sticking out of the side and pulled myself up. Then I reached up as high as I could and just barely managed to touch the top. Good thing I've got big muscles, because I was able to P-U-L-L myself up.

I was there! It was like climbing Mount McKinley, the tallest mountain peak in the United States! (Ask Mrs. Brisbane.)

I quickly pushed the switch. I wished I had some sunglasses, because I was suddenly surrounded by blinding light. It was like being inside a lightbulb.

I took the newspaper clipping out of my mouth and carefully laid it on the flat glass. Then I looked up at the wall and NO-NO-NO! Up on the screen was a picture of a car and behind it there was jumbled up backward writing! I realized I must have laid the clipping on the glass upside down. I quickly turned it over and there it was: all the information about the Moonlighters Club right there on the wall, with the outline of the car behind it.

Aldo would be coming soon, so I hurried back to the cage. It was faster getting back, because it was mostly downhill until the very end, when I had to swing my way up the cord to the blinds and back to the table.

I was panting pretty hard by the time I closed the

cage door behind me. I didn't even have time to catch my breath before Aldo swung the door open.

"Whoa! Who left that on?" he exclaimed as he entered. "That thing could overheat."

He hurried over to the overhead projector.

"Look at the wall! Look up at the wall!" I squeaked, but the words only sounded like hamster peeps.

Aldo didn't waste a second. He flicked the machine off. All that work for nothing!

But then a funny thing happened. Aldo turned the machine back on and looked at the wall. "What's this?" he muttered. "Why did Mrs. Brisbane have this up here? Hey, nice car!"

He squinted up at the screen. "Look, Humphrey. The Moonlighters Club. For people who work at night, like me."

And me, I thought. I was still quite exhausted from all that effort.

Aldo stared at the big ad on the wall for a while. Then he turned off the projector and went to work and never mentioned it again.

＊＊＊

Yes, I was annoyed. I had failed, but at least I had tried, which was more than I can say for one of my classmates. Yes, Sayeh Nasiri. With my own furry ears, I had heard her promise Mrs. Brisbane that she would raise her hand in class. But so far, she'd been as silent as a statue. Her week was almost up. Even though I'd scolded her the day she fed me, she paid no more attention to me than she had to her teacher.

You should really listen to your teacher. Even Mrs. Brisbane.

And you should always listen to your hamster.

I was worried about Aldo and about Sayeh. But I have to admit, my journey had been so tiring that—nocturnal or not—I slept soundly the rest of the night.

The next day began in a very surprising way.

"I have something to share with you all," Mrs. Brisbane announced. She held up a postcard with a picture of colorful parrots perched in lush green trees. "A postcard from Ms. McNamara." (Mrs. Brisbane would never call her Ms. Mac.) "It says:

"Greetings to my favorite class in the world, Room 26!

"I am now working in a school here in Brazil. This country is beautiful and friendly. I really enjoyed talking with the parrots in the rain forest. I miss you all, especially my pal Humphrey. Lots of love, Ms. Mac."

(Mrs. Brisbane had to say Ms. Mac since that's the way the card was signed.)

HAPPY-HAPPY-HAPPY! Not only did Ms. Mac remember me, she missed me most of all. Oh, and I missed her most of all, too. Especially every time I looked at Mrs. Brisbane and she glared back at me.

Mrs. Brisbane showed us Brazil on the map and it's far away. I'd like to be that far away from Mrs. Brisbane.

My head was so filled with memories of Ms. Mac that I only got 75% on my vocabulary test.

After we graded the tests in class, Mrs. Brisbane said, "If you got 100% on the test, please raise your hand."

That woke me up. What a clever way to get Sayeh to raise her hand. Because she always got 100%.

A.J. raised his hand. Art raised his hand.

Sayeh just stared down at her desktop.

I was starting to get really mad at her.

When it was time for map work, Mrs. Brisbane clicked on the overhead projector and there it was: the Moonlighters Club ad right on the wall. Mrs. Brisbane wrinkled her nose, picked up the paper and looked at both sides. Then she held it up to the light and I think maybe she noticed those little, tiny holes my teeth had made when I carried it over there.

Mrs. Brisbane looked over at my cage and wrinkled her nose again. Then she crumpled the paper and threw it into the wastebasket.

She's smart, but she is also *mean.*

She's not the only one. While she went on with her map work, Wait-for-the-Bell-Garth Tugwell started making some *very rude* noises.

Mrs. Brisbane didn't even turn around. When someone started giggling, she just said, "Stop-Giggling-Gail."

So Garth's rude noises got louder and even ruder. And a lot of other kids giggled along with Gail.

Suddenly, the teacher spun around to face them.

"Very well. The whole class will stay in during recess for extra vocabulary words," she announced.

Everybody groaned. "It's Garth's fault," said Heidi.

"Raise your hand," Mrs. Brisbane snapped back. "You will all stay in during recess. *Unless* the person making those noises wants to step forward and admit it."

Nobody said a word, but everybody glared at Garth, including me.

"Okay, I did it," he said.

"Raise your hand," Heidi whispered loudly.

"Very well, Garth. You, Heidi and Gail will stay in during recess," the teacher said firmly.

Heidi and Gail protested until the bell rang, but all three of them stayed in during recess. Instead of making them do extra vocabulary words, though, Mrs. Brisbane let them rest their heads on their desks. *After* she lectured them about their behavior, of course.

All this commotion had made me a little hungry, and for some reason, I hadn't been fed yet. So I decided to squeak up for myself.

Mrs. Brisbane turned and pointed at me angrily. "I don't need any trouble out of you, either," she said.

Heidi raised her hand. "I don't think he's been fed today," she said.

Mrs. Brisbane told Garth to feed me. Then she dismissed the girls and told them to go outside and play for the rest of recess.

So she wasn't completely mean to them, anyway.

She even trusted Garth to be alone in the room while she took some papers down to the office.

I'd always liked Wait-for-the-Bell-Garth, so I was surprised when he started grumbling at me as he filled the water bottle and put some fresh mealworms in my cage.

"One of these days, you'll get in trouble, too," he said. "I'll see to that."

"Huh?" I squeaked.

"Everybody hates me. Everybody loves you. You're just a rat in disguise."

The words hurt me a lot. Why would Garth say that? I mean, sure, almost everybody *does* love me, but I don't make rude noises and get other people into trouble.

I was still pondering Garth's behavior when my classmates returned to Room 26. Mrs. Brisbane must have gotten rested up over the recess, because she greeted them with a smile. "I have a surprise for you," she told the kids.

Surprises always get the class's attention. They think surprises are always good. However, I know that surprises can sometimes be bad, like the day Ms. Mac left me forever.

"We're going to pick who gets to take Humphrey home for the weekend," she explained. "Now, you all know whether or not your parents gave permission for you to bring him home. So, if you'd like Humphrey this weekend, raise your hand now."

HEY-HEY-HEY. You should have seen all the hands that went up. I could hardly believe my eyes. Miranda and Heidi and A.J. and . . . Every single hand in the class, except Garth's. Even Sayeh Nasiri raised her hand.

Mrs. Brisbane noticed.

"Sayeh, do you think it will be all right with your parents?" she asked.

Sayeh nodded her head.

"I can't hear you," said Mrs. Brisbane.

"Yes, ma'am," said Sayeh.

It was strange to hear her voice in the classroom.

Mrs. Brisbane gave her a note to bring back from her family on Friday.

I napped the rest of the afternoon, but whenever I woke up and glanced over at Sayeh's desk, I saw her doing something I'd never seen before.

Smiling.

TIP SIX: You can leave your hamster alone for a day or two. Otherwise, find a suitable caretaker, or if possible, take your hamster with you. In its own cage, a hamster can be very portable.

Guide to the Care and Feeding of Hamsters, Dr. Harvey H. Hammer

Sayeh Speaks Up

On Friday afternoon, Sayeh's father, Mr. Nasiri, picked us up after school. He had a friendly smile and gentle eyes, but he was as quiet as his daughter.

Sayeh lived in a tall building, so Mr. Nasiri carried my cage up one, two, three flights of stairs to their clean and quiet apartment.

Mrs. Nasiri opened the door for us. She spoke to her husband and daughter, but I couldn't exactly understand what they were saying.

"Hummy! Hummy!" a little voice called out.

Sayeh's little brother, Darek, toddled toward the door to greet me.

"Say *Humphrey,*" Sayeh gently corrected him.

"Hummy," he said.

The Nasiris put my cage in the living room, right in the middle of a big table. Then they pulled up chairs so they could all sit and stare into my cage.

It seemed as if they were waiting for something to happen, so I decided to give them a show. First I spun on my wheel for a while. Then I climbed up the side of the cage and dived down into a pile of soft paper.

They were obviously impressed with my performance as they talked quietly. The funny thing is, I couldn't understand a word they were saying. No wonder Sayeh got 100% on all her vocabulary tests. She and her family knew a lot more words than I did.

They finally went to the kitchen to eat dinner. Later, while the rest of the family watched television, Sayeh's mother quietly sat by my cage, watching me. She seemed NICE-NICE-NICE.

Eventually, it was bedtime for the Nasiris. But after the lights were out, Sayeh slipped out of her room and came back to my cage and whispered to me. I could understand her again.

"Now you know my secret, Humphrey," she whispered. "My family doesn't speak English. Well, my dad does a little, but he's shy about it. Mom hasn't learned any English at all. And Darek's too little."

"I understand," I squeaked.

"That's why I don't like to talk in class," she explained. "I don't talk like the other kids. I'm afraid they'll laugh at my accent. That happened to me when I was little."

"But you don't sound different," I frantically squeaked. "I understand you just fine."

Unfortunately, she didn't understand me. All she heard was "Squeak-squeak-squeak." I guess maybe I have an accent, too.

"But I have an idea that maybe you could help me teach Mom English," Sayeh continued.

"Glad to help out if I can," I squeaked to her.

"You're a real friend," Sayeh replied.

See? She understood me after all.

The next day, I dozed until late afternoon, when Sayeh led her mother back to my cage.

"Humphrey only understands English, Mama," Sayeh said. "Speak English. Say 'Humphrey.' "

Sayeh's mom looked a little frightened, but she tried.

"Hum-freee," she said.

"Hummy," Darek cried as he raced into the room and climbed onto his mother's lap.

"Say, 'Hello, Humphrey,' " Sayeh gently instructed her mother.

"Hel-lo, Hump-free," Mrs. Nasiri said.

I squeaked, "Hello," right back and she broke into a huge smile.

"Hello," she said.

"Good job," I said.

Well, things went swimmingly from then on. In a matter of hours, Sayeh's mom was saying, "How do you do?" "Nice to meet you." "Would you like some water?" (I did, thank you.)

Even when Sayeh and Darek left to go to the store with their father, Mrs. Nasiri kept on talking. I let her know I understood what she was saying by wiggling my whiskers and hanging by one paw from the top of my cage.

"Good boy, Humphrey," she said.

Sayeh and her father were amazed at Mrs. Nasiri's progress when they returned. The family spent the rest of the evening practicing English.

First, Sayeh pretended to be a guest at the door. She went into the hall and knocked.

Her mother opened the door. "Hello, Sayeh," she said. "Won't you come in?"

Then Darek went out and knocked. Mrs. Nasiri opened the door and said, "Hello, Darek. Won't you come in?"

He rushed in and toddled right over to the table, shouting, "Humfy! Humfy!"

Next, Sayeh convinced her dad to practice English with her mom.

"What time it is?" asked Mrs. Nasiri.

"What time is it?" Sayeh corrected her.

Mrs. Nasiri got it right the second time. Then Dad looked at his watch. "Seven-fifteen," he answered.

"Would you like some tea?" Mrs. Nasiri asked.

"Yes, please. I would like some tea," Mr. Nasiri answered.

Guess what? They had a tea party right on my table.

As a reward for all their hard work, I spun my wheel as fast as my legs would go, and they all cheered.

Later, after the lights were out, Sayeh slipped out of her room to talk to me again.

"Thank you, Humphrey," she whispered. "My mom says she's ready to go to English class now. But I wish you were the teacher."

"So do I," I squeaked, and I meant it.

There were more English lessons on Sunday and Sayeh showed Darek how to clean out my cage. Suddenly, the boy began to giggle.

"Humphrey poop!" he yelled. His English was improving, too.

On Sunday night, Sayeh gathered her family together again.

"I want to teach you the American song," she said. Then she opened her mouth and began to sing, "Oh, say, can you see? By the dawn's early light."

I stood up, just like we do in the classroom when "The Star-Spangled Banner" is being sung. But I'd never heard it sung like that before. Sayeh had the most beautiful voice in the world! It was like a gentle breeze . . . no, like rippling waters . . . no, it was . . . well, it was beautiful.

If only our classmates in Room 26 could hear her!

Which gave me the start of another idea. But I didn't have time to think much at all. Because soon, the whole family was singing "The Star-Spangled Banner," and I squeaked right along with them! Even on those high notes.

When we got back to school on Monday morning, though, I was a little disappointed. Mrs. Brisbane asked Sayeh how things went over the weekend.

"Fine," said Sayeh. And nothing more.

Like Ms. Mac said, "You can learn a lot about yourself by getting to know another species." But boy, sometimes it's a lot of work.

That Monday, I sat in my cage worrying about Sayeh

for quite a while before I dozed off. When I woke up, I noticed that Room 26 had changed. The bulletin board was covered with brightly colored leaves. The tops of the chalkboards were lined with big paper witches, ghosts and skeletons. Hanging from the light fixtures were black crepe-paper bats. Then I looked to my right and gasped. A horrible, huge orange face with an evil grin was staring directly at me. I jumped back, my heart pounding.

"Hey, Humphrey, don't you like old pumpkin head?" A.J. whispered to me from his seat nearby.

"Look! Humphrey's scared of a little old jack-o'-lantern," Garth said. "Scaredy-cat. Scaredy-hamster."

I stood up straight and looked as un-scared as I possibly could.

"Quiet, Garth and A.J.," said Mrs. Brisbane. Then she quickly returned to a math problem she was writing on the board.

Suddenly, I noticed a little movement in the center of the room. A murmur. A change. I looked over and YES-YES-YES! Sayeh had her hand up. Everyone noticed it, except Mrs. Brisbane, who had her back to the rest of us.

"Mrs. Brisbane?" Heidi called out.

Without turning, the teacher said, "Raise-Your-Hand-Heidi."

Now Heidi had her hand raised as well as Sayeh.

"Well, what is it?" Mrs. Brisbane turned to face the class and was obviously surprised at what she saw.

"Yes, Sayeh," she said.

In a loud, clear voice, Sayeh said, "May I move the pumpkin away from Humphrey's cage?"

Mrs. Brisbane looked from Sayeh to the cage and back.

"Yes. I guess it is a little close. Thank you, Sayeh."

Sayeh rose and hurried to my table to push the ugly old jack-o'-lantern away. She didn't say a word, but she winked at me and I knew what she meant.

"Heidi, did you want to say something?" Mrs. Brisbane asked.

"Not anymore," she said.

Everything went back to normal until the bell rang for recess. As my classmates all scattered and ran toward the door, Garth paused by my cage.

"Scaredy-cat," he muttered. Then he moved the pumpkin right up against my cage again.

I puffed up my cheeks as big as I could get them. It was going to be a very long day.

TIP SEVEN: When hamsters feel intimidated, they often puff up their cheeks.

Guide to the Care and Feeding of Hamsters, Dr. Harvey H. Hammer

Tricks and Treats

allow-Een. Or Hollowin'. Or Howloween.

I wasn't sure what it was, but I was pretty sure I didn't like it.

Especially on Monday night, after Mrs. Brisbane turned out the lights. That's when those skeletons on the wall took on an eerie glow.

The bats hanging from the ceiling began to whirl and twirl.

And the smile on that ghastly orange pumpkin face looked more like a wicked smirk.

WEIRD-WEIRD-WEIRD.

So I was thrilled when Aldo flicked on the lights.

"Whoa. It looks like Halloween in here," he exclaimed as he wheeled in his cleaning cart. He strolled over to my cage as usual and bent down so we were face-to-face.

"So, are you going to wear a costume for Halloween? It's Wednesday, you know. Halloween is when the ghosts and goblins come out to play," he explained.

"Eeeek!" I squeaked.

"No, no, it's not scary. It's just fun. All the kids will wear costumes. Richie's going to be a werewolf. So what are you going to wear? A fur coat?" He laughed at his own joke, then began his cleaning routine, talking to me as he swept and dusted.

I started thinking about this costume thing. Ms. Mac had a costume party once while I was staying with her. People dressed up like kings and pirates and ghosts, and Ms. Mac dressed up like a clown with a sparkly pink wig and a funny face.

Nobody wore a fur coat.

I thought about this costume thing all night and the next day.

When Garth threw a piece of wadded-up paper in my cage, I wondered about the costumes.

When A.J. tripped on his way up to the chalkboard and Gail didn't giggle, I wondered about the costumes.

Even when Mrs. Brisbane called on Sayeh and she answered her, I wondered about the costumes.

And I came up with a Plan of my own.

On Wednesday, Halloween arrived. But there were no costumes. I was extremely disappointed until Heidi blurted out, "Mrs. Brisbane, when are we going to have the party?"

"Raise-Your-Hand-Heidi," the teacher told her.

Heidi obediently raised her hand and Mrs. Brisbane called on her. This time, when Heidi asked her question,

Mrs. Brisbane said, "We will have our lessons this morning. After lunch, you may put on your costumes and we'll start the party."

I felt HAPPY-HAPPY-HAPPY and got in a nice nap for the rest of the morning.

But I was wide-awake after lunch. My classmates returned from the cafeteria, then scurried off to the cloakroom and the bathrooms and returned. But I hardly recognized them in their costumes.

Oh, they were wonderful! A dragon, two pirates, a princess, a ninja. Two clowns, a ballerina, a bunny, a cat (thank goodness not a real one), a baseball player, a mad scientist, a skeleton, the Statue of Liberty, an angel and a devil!

The room mothers came to help with the party. They were both dressed as witches. Still, Mrs. Brisbane was the scariest of them all.

She didn't wear a costume—just a button that had the words "This IS my costume" printed on it.

She gathered everyone in a circle, pushing all the tables back. Then she announced that the class would be having some treats. But in order to get them, they each had to do a trick: tell a joke, sing a song or perform a trick for the rest of the class.

Oh, I wish someone had told me. I had figured out the costume part, but what about this tricking for treats?

Art (the ninja) stood on his head. He stood on his head so long, Mrs. Brisbane finally had to thank him and tell him it was someone else's turn.

Gail (the ballerina) twirled around the room on her toes. Garth (baseball player) told a joke about a witch. Miranda (bunny) sang a funny song about your ears hanging low. It was all very entertaining, except for the fact that I was thinking about Something Else.

But Mrs. Brisbane got my full attention when she called on Sayeh. Sayeh was dressed as the Statue of Liberty. She wore a flowing dress and had a crown on her head and a big cardboard torch in one hand. She stared down at the floor as she took her place in the center of the circle.

"What trick will you do for us, Sayeh?" the teacher asked.

Sayeh still stared at the floor.

"Sing your song, Sayeh! Sing!" I squeaked out as loudly as I could. "You can do it, Sayeh. Sing!"

Yes, I know all she could hear was "Squeak-squeak-squeak," but I did my best.

"I think Humphrey wants to hear from you," said Mrs. Brisbane in a surprisingly friendly voice.

Suddenly, without warning, Sayeh began to sing "The Star-Spangled Banner" in her clear, sweet voice.

Everyone stood up right away, like you're supposed to when they sing the national anthem. Mrs. Brisbane put her hand over her heart and the other kids did, too. Well, Pay-Attention-Art didn't until his mom came over and whispered in his ear.

I stood up, too, as proud as a hamster could possibly be.

When it was over, no one clapped or said a word. It seemed as if those sweet notes were still drifting around the room.

"That was lovely, Sayeh. Thank you for sharing your beautiful voice with us," Mrs. Brisbane said.

I wish she'd speak that way to me someday. Nice. Encouraging. Friendly.

Anyway, the tricks continued. And after A.J. told a few riddles, Mrs. Brisbane looked around the circle and said, "Did I miss anyone?"

This was the moment I'd been waiting for. No one had noticed, but the night before, I had sneaked one of Aldo's white dusting cloths into my sleeping hut. I had to act quickly. I pulled out the cloth and crawled under so it completely covered me. Then I stood up and began to shout like I'd never shouted before.

"Trick or squeak!" I cried. "Trick or squeak!"

Miranda noticed first. "Look!" she yelled. "It's Humphrey!"

I wish I could have seen the faces of my classmates, but it was DARK-DARK-DARK under the cloth. I could hear them, though. First there were gasps, then giggles, then shouts of "Look!" and "Humphrey's a ghost!"

I continued to squeak my heart out until I heard Mrs. Brisbane's firm footsteps coming toward my cage.

"Who did this?" she asked. "Who put that on Humphrey?"

No one answered, of course. Not even me.

"He could suffocate under that," she said.

"But he looks so cute," Heidi called out.

Mrs. Brisbane didn't answer. She just said, "Will someone please uncover him?"

Golden-Miranda opened the cage door and whisked the cloth away.

"Humphrey, you are a riot," she said.

Only a riot? Let's be honest here: I was a smash hit!

Then the room mothers served up cupcakes with orange icing and cups of apple juice, and my classmates played games.

Just before the bell rang, Mrs. Brisbane clapped her hands and made an announcement. "Mrs. Hopper and Mrs. Patel and I have consulted with one another. We have decided to give the prize for Best Trick to Sayeh Nasiri."

Everyone clapped and cheered as Mrs. Brisbane handed Sayeh a blue ribbon. Sayeh looked over at me and smiled a beautiful smile.

Mrs. Brisbane continued. "And we have decided to award the prize for Best Costume to . . . Humphrey."

She walked over to my cage and taped a big blue ribbon to it while my classmates cheered for me.

"Thank you," I squeaked, but I'm not sure anyone could hear me over all the noise. "Thank you all."

The bell rang and the room was soon empty, except for Mrs. Brisbane. As she gathered up her papers to take home, Mr. Morales came in. He was dressed in a cap and gown like people wear when they are graduating.

"Happy Halloween, Sue. Did you have a good party?" he asked.

"Very," she answered. "Somehow your friend over there got hold of a ghost costume and won the prize."

"See? I told you he'd add a lot to your classroom," he said with a smile.

"He has livened things up," said Mrs. Brisbane.

JOY-JOY-JOY! I believed she was starting to like me.

"Just so he doesn't liven things up too much," she added.

Poof. My hopes of winning over Mrs. Brisbane's heart crashed to the ground.

Mr. Morales said his kids kept asking about me and then he quickly left. Mrs. Brisbane headed out the door after him.

There I was, all alone in Room 26 with a bunch of half-torn bats and tattered skeletons hanging around me.

As I waited for Aldo to arrive, I sat in the darkening room and pondered my job as a classroom pet. Had I really accomplished anything? Mr. Morales's children seemed to settle down when I was there. Sayeh's mother began to learn English. And Sayeh would probably never have sung in front of the class without my encouragement.

Still, Mrs. Brisbane was not won over.

Neither was Garth Tugwell, although it seemed as if he had liked me well enough in the beginning. Now he always muttered things at me as he passed by my cage.

I noticed that he was the only one in class who didn't cheer when I won the award for Best Costume.

I was still worrying about Garth when the lights temporarily blinded me as Aldo sailed into the classroom, yelling, "Trick or treat!"

He was wearing his usual work shirt, dark pants and heavy shoes. But on his face he wore huge glasses with a bulbous nose attached. The center of the glasses had giant eyeballs painted on with circles of red veins. His floppy mustache drooped out from under the nose.

"Great costume," I squeaked.

"Hey, what's this?" Aldo rushed forward to examine my blue ribbon. "Best Costume? For a fur coat? I'll have to ask Richie about that," he said.

Aldo reached into his lunch box and pulled out a juicy slice of apple.

"I've got a special Halloween treat for you, Humphrey. 'Cause I'm very, very happy tonight," he said.

I grabbed the apple and began nibbling as Aldo pulled his chair up close to my cage.

"You see, I went to the Moonlighters Club. You remember, the club in that ad I found on the projector?"

I squeaked an excited "Yes."

"And I met a real nice girl there, named Maria. She works all night at the bakery. So tomorrow, we're going out on a date. Lunch and a movie." Aldo leaned back in his chair.

"She's a real nice girl. Pretty. Nice. Did I tell you she works in a bakery?"

Aldo rose and paced back and forth in front of my cage.

"You know what I can't figure? I can't figure out how that ad got on that projector. Mrs. Brisbane wouldn't show that to the class. And she wouldn't be interested herself. And it was weird how the projector was left on. Mrs. Brisbane always leaves her room in shipshape condition." He paused to rub his chin, then looked at me out of the corner of his eye.

"You know, if you weren't locked up in a cage, I'd think you had something to do with it," he said. Then he laughed. "Well, whoever it was, I owe them a big thank-you."

"You're welcome," I squeaked.

Too bad Aldo didn't understand me this time.

TIP EIGHT: Hamsters are most active during the evening.
Guide to the Care and Feeding of Hamsters, Dr. Harvey H. Hammer

The Art of Self-Defense

O kay, I was having a great week, no doubt about it. Not only did I get the blue ribbon on Wednesday, but on Thursday the class got a long letter from Ms. Mac. She included a picture of her standing by a waterfall next to some very strange-looking creatures. They looked like hairy pigs or racoony dogs.

"These are coatis," Mrs. Brisbane said, reading from the letter. "Pronounced *ko-ahh-tees.*"

The coatis looked weird. Ms. Mac looked gorgeous, especially with all the red, yellow and orange flowers surrounding her.

How I wished I could be there with her! Except maybe for the fact that those coatis might not be hamster-friendly.

At the end of her letter, Ms. Mac wrote, "So farewell to all my wonderful friends in Room 26, especially the small one with the big heart: Humphrey."

SIGH-SIGH-SIGH.

Though the thought of Ms. Mac made me happy, the

weekend was coming up soon and I always felt a little nervous about where I'd be spending it.

When it was decided on Thursday that I was going home with Golden-Miranda—I mean Miranda Golden—I was so excited, I only got an 83% on my vocabulary test. (Sayeh got 100%. I know, because this time when Mrs. Brisbane asked who got 100%, she raised her hand.)

I always figured that Miranda lived in a castle, because she reminded me of a fairy-tale princess in disguise. Wherever it was, it had to be wonderful if Miranda lived there.

Well, Miranda's home wasn't exactly a castle, but it was very tall. Miranda lived in a fourth-floor apartment with her mom and her big dog, Clem. We had to take an elevator to get there.

The apartment was nice. The mom was nice. Clem was not nice.

Let me explain. Miranda has a small bedroom and her mom let me stay there, right on the desk. To welcome me, the two of them did a complete cleanout of my cage. "I'll bet nobody's done this for a while," said Miranda's mom, and she was right. Pretty soon, I felt like a brand-new hamster!

Suddenly, Clem bounded into the room, a big mass of yellow fur poking his huge nose right up against my cage. His wet nostrils were like two eyes staring in at me and he stuck out a giant tongue that came at me like a tidal wave. Luckily, the cage protected me.

"Mom!" Miranda yelled. "Please get Clem out of here!"

Thank heavens Mom took Clem out for a walk in the park while Miranda showed me her room. She held pictures of her friends and family up to the cage so I could see. Her dad. Her stepmom. Her grandparents in Florida.

Next, she introduced me to her goldfish, Fanny. She wasn't much of a conversationalist. I squeaked, "Nice to meet you, Fanny," and she said, "Blub."

I was thinking about how wonderful it would be to live with Miranda all the time when Clem returned from the park and galloped into the room.

"Clem, stay out!" Miranda shouted. But Clem just wagged his tail and barked.

Miranda closed the door so the dog had to stay outside, but we could still hear him whining and crying like a baby out in the hall.

Still, just being with Miranda made everything seem golden until her mom called her to go shopping. Miranda protested. Good girl! But Mom didn't want her to stay inside on such a nice day. She had no choice, unless she was rude to her mom, which Miranda never would be!

"I won't be gone long," Miranda told me. "And I'll make sure the door is shut tightly so Clem can't get in."

Everything would be all right, I assured myself. After all, Miranda had said so. I was all set to get in a good day-time snooze.

But as soon as the door to the apartment closed, Clem started whining outside the room. I could hear his big paws up on the door, trying to push it open. I was a little nervous, but Miranda had assured me I'd be all right. After all, she wouldn't be gone long.

Then I heard it, the slight turning of the doorknob as Clem flung himself at the door repeatedly. What a barbarian he was.

Suddenly, the door swung open and Clem burst in and ran straight to my cage.

I tried to distract him by spinning on my wheel. I can do that for hours, if necessary. I thought the spinning wheel might even hypnotize him, like in an old movie I'd seen with Ms. Mac. (Ms. Mac! Where was she when I needed her?)

But apparently all that spinning just excited Clem more. He started barking at me, but I couldn't understand a word he said.

"Now cut that out!" I squeaked at him. That just seemed to make him more hot and bothered.

He plopped his front paws up on the desk and stuck his nose against the cage door, near the lock.

The lock-that-doesn't-lock.

"Easy now. Calm down." I squeaked soothingly at the beast, but he kept poking his nose at the cage, showing me his huge tongue and the huge teeth around it.

(Let me just say that Clem could stand some breath mints.)

He poked the lock again and again. I knew if he jiggled it enough, the door would swing open and I'd be history. Poor Miranda would never know what had happened to me. She might even cry. I couldn't stand the thought of Miranda crying. I hopped back on my wheel and started spinning with all my might, hoping to buy some time.

Clem pulled back for a moment and stared at the wheel going round and round.

(Let me just say I'm glad that Clem is about two quarts low in the brain department.)

Whew, I'm a good spinner, but I was getting worried about how long I could keep it up when Golden-Miranda rushed in. She never looked more beautiful to me than at that moment.

"Clem! Stop it!" she shouted in a very firm voice. "Bad boy!"

Clem raced to her side, wagging his tail.

Miranda's mom dragged old Clem out of the room and closed the door behind her.

WHEW-WHEW-WHEW!

Miranda was very sorry. She opened the cage and reached in to pick me up. "Poor Humphrey," she said, hugging me. She set me on her desk and stroked me gently with one finger. "I'm so sorry, Humphrey. So sorry."

Ohhhhh. I don't know what felt better: the petting or Miranda's soothing words.

Miranda felt so terrible about what had happened, she let me play on her desk. She lined up books all along the edges so I wouldn't fall off. Then she let me wander around and see the sights.

A desktop is a very interesting place, in case you've

never explored one. Miranda's desktop had a big cup with hearts all over it. The cup was filled with pencils. Ah, pencils smell so sweet. She had a round silvery container of paper clips and a square purple container of rubber bands. She had lots of paper in a pink box. And she had a great big fat dictionary. I could really use one of those. I wonder if they make doll-sized dictionaries you can hide behind a hamster's mirror?

Miranda giggled as she watched me check things out. When I tried to climb into the paper clip box, she stopped me with her finger.

"No, no, Humphrey. Those would hurt you."

She did the same thing when I tried to roll in the rubber band box.

"No, Humphrey. Rubber bands can be very dangerous," she told me.

Well, I guess I knew *that*. Hadn't Garth shot a rubber band at A.J. last week and almost got sent to Principal Morales's office? Hadn't A.J. held his arm and said, "Ow," when the rubber band hit him?

Anyway, I really enjoyed my time on the desk, until I heard Clem barking. Then I made a beeline for home.

"Oh, Humphrey, I won't let Clem hurt you. Honest," Miranda assured me as she gently helped me back in my cage.

I believed her. I really did.

But when it was bedtime and Miranda's mom came into the room to say good night, she said some words that sent a chill up my spine.

"Don't forget, we're going to the Nicolsons' house tomorrow night."

Miranda protested. "I hate to leave Humphrey. Clem gives him such a hard time."

"We'll lock the door this time, honey. He'll be okay," her mom said. "And tonight, Clem will be in my room."

After her mother left, Miranda assured me that Clem loves to sleep in Mom's room. "But if anything happens and you get scared, just give me a squeak," she told me.

"Don't worry, I will!" I assured her.

I didn't sleep that night. For one thing, the stars on Miranda's ceiling glow in the dark and they're so beautiful, I couldn't take my eyes off them.

For another thing . . . well, I am nocturnal.

But mainly I didn't sleep because I was worried about Clem.

After my experience that afternoon, I believed that no lock could hold him back. And how could a little hamster fight back? What weapon would I have against a big, hairy, bad-breathed, small-brained creature?

What weapon, indeed! I had an Idea.

Clem hadn't made a peep for hours, so I took a chance and quietly opened the lock-that-doesn't-lock and dashed across the desktop to pick my weapon, just in case of another encounter with Clem. Then I scampered back to the cage with it and quietly closed the door.

I hid my weapon behind my mirror, next to the notebook, where no one could find it. Then I managed to get forty winks or so of sleep around sunrise.

Miranda and her mom kept Clem out of my sight all day, until it was time for them to go to their party.

"I'm still worried," said Miranda.

"I'm locking your door with a key on the outside," her mom said. "I'm locking Clem in my room. And Humphrey's cage is closed tightly. Right?"

Miranda checked it. Everybody always checks it. It always seems locked from the outside. It even makes a clicking sound. But from the inside, believe me, it's a piece of cake to open.

Miranda seemed satisfied with the arrangement, but I wasn't. So I remained on high alert all that afternoon and evening. And here's what happened.

After Miranda and her mom left, Clem barked for a while.

Then I heard jiggling and joggling for about an hour.

Next, I heard big hairy feet padding down the hall toward Miranda's room. Toward *my* room.

I sucked in my breath and waited. Yes, I knew Miranda's mom had locked the door with a key. But Clem didn't seem to let little things like that stand in his way.

The doorknob squeaked and rattled. It twisted and turned. Nothing happened. But that didn't seem to bother Clem the barbarian.

He jiggled-rattled-and-twisted it some more. When he got tired of that, he threw his whole body at the door.

And then, very slowly, the door opened.

Clem actually seemed surprised, but I wasn't. I had spent the last two hours carefully preparing for this moment.

Not that my heart wasn't going THUMP-THUMP-THUMP very loudly. Even Fanny the fish seemed nervous.

Clem trotted right up to my cage and stuck his big wet nose up against it.

"Stay away! Keep your distance!" I squeaked. "I'm warning you."

Clem wasn't discouraged one bit.

"Woof!" he barked, sending a foul cloud of doggy breath my way.

I didn't even flinch.

He barked a few more times and then began poking his big nose against the cage door. I wondered if he actually knew the lock was broken.

The time had arrived to put my Plan into action. I was in grave danger and I had no choice. I would only have one chance at Clem because I only had one weapon: a rubber band. It had taken me a long time to get it hooked around the edge of my food dish. Now I carefully pulled it back as far as I could, aiming directly at those big doggy nostrils.

"You asked for it, beast!" I squeaked.

Then I let loose. The rubber band snapped and sailed through the air, hitting Clem squarely on the nose.

He yelped like a baby and raced out of the room as if he'd seen a ghost. Too bad I didn't still have my ghost costume. That would have been a nice touch.

I guess Clem wasn't quite as dumb as I had thought, because he never even tried to come back in the room again.

Of course, Miranda and her mom were really puzzled when they came home and found both bedrooms unlocked and Clem cowering under the living-room sofa.

"I don't get it," said Miranda. "Humphrey looks just fine. Maybe it was a burglar."

But Miranda's mom checked the closets and drawers, and nothing was missing.

"Now, that's a mystery," said Miranda's mother after she'd searched the whole apartment.

Miranda stared at me, shaking her head.

"If only Humphrey could talk," she said.

"But I *can* if you'd just listen," I told her.

"I bet you'd have a lot to tell us," Miranda continued, not understanding my squeaks.

Yes, I do, I thought. Enough to fill a book.

TIP NINE: Hamsters do not enjoy contact with other animals. A cat or dog may eat a hamster or at least do it bodily harm.

Guide to the Care and Feeding of Hamsters, Dr. Harvey H. Hammer

10

Garth Versus A.J.

"If you have dogs or cats, you have to be very careful not to let them get near Humphrey," Miranda warned the rest of the class when we returned to Room 26.

"You can say that again," I squeaked. But she didn't.

I still considered Golden-Miranda to be a special friend and I had a very clean cage to show for my weekend, as well as a new respect for rubber bands. But I also decided that even though Miranda is practically a perfect person, I was not in a hurry to stay with her again.

A.J. raised his hand and Mrs. Brisbane called on him.

"May I have Humphrey this weekend? We don't have a dog or a cat," he bellowed.

"Lower-Your-Voice-A.J. I'll let you know on Thursday. There may be other students who want Humphrey as well."

At least half the hands in the classroom went up as kids started shouting, "Me, me!" I was quite flattered. But for some reason, the whole subject seemed to make Garth mad.

Within minutes, he shot a rubber band at A.J.

"Ouch!" A.J. complained loudly. When he told the teacher what had happened, Garth denied it.

"Humphrey did it," he said.

Gail giggled. Mrs. Brisbane did not. "I don't believe a hamster can shoot a rubber band," she said sternly. A lot she knows!

The next day, Garth stuck his foot out and tripped Art as he went to sharpen his pencil.

"I didn't do it! He's just clumsy," Garth protested when Mrs. Brisbane angrily scolded him.

That same day, Garth pushed Gail at morning recess. He spent afternoon recess inside.

"Garth Tugwell, you're halfway to Principal Morales's office right now." Mrs. Brisbane sounded really angry.

Garth just shrugged his shoulders.

On Wednesday, Garth sneaked back into the room while Mrs. Brisbane went to the office during recess, and he headed straight for my cage. The two of us were all alone in the room.

"Hello, rat. Why don't you just run away? Then nobody will take you home on the weekend," he said. He opened my cage door and grabbed me. "You'd like your freedom, wouldn't you, rat?"

He set me on the floor. My heart was pounding. THUMP-THUMP-THUMP!

"Go on, rat. Skedaddle." He gave me a little push with his hand.

I scampered under the table. I wanted to say something, but for the first time ever, I was scared squeakless.

"Have fun," he said, and in an instant he was gone.

I was pretty confused. For one thing, I didn't want to run away. I was perfectly happy staying in Room 26 and having adventures on the weekend.

Where would I go? What would I do?

There was no time to waste. I scampered over to the cord that hung down from the blinds and grabbed on to it. Then I started the old swinging routine, back and forth, swinging a little higher each time until I reached the tabletop. Back-forth-back-forth-back-forth . . . leap! There wasn't time to think about my queasy stomach as I raced into my cage, slamming the door shut behind me.

Just then, Mrs. Brisbane returned. I darted into my sleeping house so she wouldn't see how hard I was breathing.

I saw her look at the window, puzzled. She walked over to it and stared at the blind cord, which was still swinging. She reached out and stopped it with her hand. Then she shook her head and walked away.

When recess was over and my classmates filed back into the class, Garth looked over at my cage, half smiling. But that smile quickly disappeared when he saw that the door was closed. He leaped out of his seat and looked in my cage.

"Howdy," I squeaked at him.

"Garth, please get back in your seat," Mrs. Brisbane told him.

"But Humphrey!" he protested.

"Well, what is it?" Mrs. Brisbane was getting irritated.

"He's in his cage!" he said.

A few of my classmates giggled, but not Mrs. Brisbane.

"In case you haven't noticed, he's always in his cage, Garth," she said. "Now get back in your seat."

Garth did what she said, but for the rest of the day I noticed him staring over at me.

On Thursday, Mrs. Brisbane announced that I would be spending the weekend at A.J.'s house.

"Yes!" shouted A.J., delighted at the news.

A few seconds later, a whole series of rubber bands hit A.J. on his neck, shoulder and head.

"Cool it, Garth!" yelled A.J., jumping out of his chair. "Man, I'm tired of these rubber bands."

Garth acted innocent. "I don't know where they came from. They could have come from anywhere."

"Garth did it," Heidi said. "I saw him."

Mrs. Brisbane didn't remind Heidi to raise her hand. But she did tell Garth to stay in during recess.

"Not fair," Garth muttered under his breath.

When the bell rang for recess, Garth stayed in his seat. Mrs. Brisbane closed the door when all the other students had left and walked to his desk. Normally, I would have been napping at this time, but I was wide-awake and wondering what that boy had to say.

"Garth. You've been acting strangely lately. You never got into trouble at all until two weeks ago. Now you're shooting rubber bands at people and disturbing the entire class. Can you tell me why?"

Garth slowly shook his head no.

"Your grades are slipping, too. Has something changed in your life?"

Garth slowly shook his head again.

"How about at home? Is anything wrong?"

Garth didn't shake his head. He didn't move a muscle.

"Should I talk to your parents about your behavior, Garth?"

Garth's face got very red.

"No," he said with a choking sound.

Mrs. Brisbane moved closer and put her hand on Garth's shoulder. "Tell me what's wrong."

"My . . . mom's . . . sick," he said. "Real sick." Tears ran down his cheeks. I was feeling a little teary-eyed myself.

"How sick?" Mrs. Brisbane asked.

"She lost all this weight and she was in and out of the hospital and now she's just tired all the time and . . ." Garth didn't try to finish his sentence.

Garth wiped away the tears with the tissue Mrs. Brisbane handed him. "That's why I can't take Humphrey home. My dad says we can't let anything bother Mom. Well, my little brother bothers her and we let him in the house."

Mrs. Brisbane smiled slightly. "Humphrey is a big responsibility, Garth. That's why I don't take him home. My husband's been sick, too. Did you know that?"

Garth shook his head. "No."

"So I know what it's like. Listen, I'll make a few calls tonight. Maybe we can find a way for you to spend some time with Humphrey," she said.

"But he hates me," I squeaked.

"I'd like to," said Garth.

Huh? I was confused.

"But you have to promise me that you won't disrupt the class anymore," Mrs. Brisbane told him. "Is that a deal?"

Garth nodded. "Deal."

As you know, I'm very good at coming up with plans to solve human problems. Very, very good. But try as I might, I couldn't imagine what Mrs. Brisbane's plan to get Garth to spend time with me could be.

I was still trying to figure it out when Aldo arrived that night.

"Humphrey, my man!" he yelled when he opened the door.

I almost fell off my wheel.

"You are the most handsome, intelligent hamster in the world! And I am the luckiest man in the world! Because I am dating the most beautiful woman in the world!"

Aldo swept his way toward my cage, then lowered his voice. "Uh, but don't tell anybody I said so. Not yet. After all, Maria and I have only been out three times. But, oh, what times we've had!"

He pulled up a chair and sat very close to me.

"And it's all thanks to the Moonlighters Club. And that clipping over there. . . ." He pointed toward the spot where the overhead projector had once stood. "And you! I know you had something to do with it. I just can't figure out what. Anyway, don't tell anybody, but someday, I'm going to marry Maria. And when I do, I want you to be best man. Or best hamster, I guess. I really mean it. If you were a guy, I'd buy you a burger."

He reached in his pocket and pulled out a little piece of foil. "Instead, I got you this." He unwrapped a piece of carrot and put it in my cage.

"Thank you, Aldo," I squeaked. "I wish you lots of happiness."

"I knew you'd be happy for me, Humphrey." Aldo smiled and then jumped up. "Whooo! I've got so much energy, I can clean this room in half the time. I could climb a mountain and not even get tired! I could conquer the world!" He leaned forward and grinned through his glorious mustache. "Ain't love grand?"

"If you say so," I replied.

I'd never seen anyone so happy before. The only thing that would make me that happy would be if Ms. Mac came back.

She's not coming back.

And I'm still stuck with Mrs. Brisbane. And she's stuck with me.

Say, what did she mean when she said she doesn't take me home because her husband's sick? Did she mean she *would* take me home if her husband wasn't sick?

I thought about it all night and came up with this answer: NO-NO-NO.

She doesn't take me home because she doesn't like me.

Maybe I'm lucky after all.

TIP TEN: Hamsters are incredible acrobats and climbers. They seem to defy the laws of gravity.

Guide to the Care and Feeding of Hamsters, Dr. Harvey H. Hammer

TV or Not TV

Wow! Friday was a great adventure because A.J. took me on the school bus. It was noisy and smelly and very, very bumpy, and just about everyone on the bus wanted to get a good look at me, including the driver, Miss Victoria.

It was exciting—almost too exciting because A.J. couldn't hold my cage steady and I was slipping and sliding and bouncing until I was quite dizzy.

"Sorry, Humphrey. I'm trying to hold still," A.J. told me as someone bumped his elbow and sent me sprawling on the floor of my cage.

"It's all right," I squeaked weakly.

The bus let us off close to A.J.'s house. It was a two-story old house with a big porch. As soon as I entered, I got a warm welcome from A.J.'s mom, his younger brother, Ty, his little sister, DeeLee, and his baby brother, Beau.

"Anthony James, introduce us to your little friend," his mom said, greeting us.

Anthony James? Everybody at school called A.J. by his initials or just "Aje."

"This is Humphrey," he answered.

"Hello, Humphrey," said Mrs. Thomas. "So how was your day, Anthony?"

"Lousy. Garth kept shooting rubber bands at me. He won't leave me alone."

"But you two used to be friends," his mother said.

"Used to be," said A.J. "Until he turned into a JERK."

Mom patted her son on the shoulder. "Well, you've got the whole weekend to get over it. Now take Humphrey into the den and get him settled."

Mrs. Brisbane called him Lower-Your-Voice-A.J. because A.J. always talked extra loud in class. I soon noticed that everybody at A.J.'s house talked extra loud. They had to, because in the background the TV was always blaring.

Now, every house I've been in so far has had a TV. Even Ms. Mac had a TV, and I enjoyed some of the shows I'd seen with her.

There's one channel that has nothing but the most frightening shows about wild animals attacking one another. I mean *wild,* like tigers and bears and hippopotamuses. (Gee, I hope that's not on our vocabulary test in the near future.) Those shows make me appreciate the protection of a nice cage. As long as the lock doesn't quite lock.

There's another channel that only has people in funny-looking clothes dancing and singing in very strange places. It makes me glad that I have a fur coat and don't have to figure out what to wear every day.

Mostly, I like the cartoon shows. Sometimes they have mice and rabbits and other interesting rodents, although I've never seen a hamster show. Yet.

Anyway, the difference at the Thomases' house is that the television is on *all the time*. There's a TV on a table across from a big comfy couch and a big comfy chair and someone's almost always sitting there watching. I know because they put my cage down on the floor next to the couch. I had a very good view of the TV.

I couldn't always hear the TV, though, because A.J.'s mother had a radio in the kitchen, which was blaring most of the time while she cooked or did crossword puzzles or talked on the phone. No matter what she did, the radio was always on.

When A.J.'s dad came home from work, he plopped down on the couch and watched TV while he played with the baby. Then A.J. and Ty plugged in some video games and played while Dad watched. DeeLee listened to the radio with her mom and danced around the kitchen.

When it was time for dinner, the whole family took plates and sat in the den so they could watch TV while they ate.

Then they watched TV some more. They made popcorn and kept watching.

Finally, the kids went to bed. The baby first, then DeeLee and later Ty and A.J.

After they were all in their rooms, Mr. and Mrs. Thomas kept watching TV and ate some ice cream.

Later, Mrs. Thomas yawned loudly. "I've had it, Charlie. I'm going to bed and I suggest you do, too," she said.

But Mr. Thomas just kept on watching. Or at least he kept on sitting there until he fell asleep on the couch. I ended up watching the rest of the wrestling match without him. Unfortunately, the wrestler I was rooting for, Thor of Glore, lost. Finally, Mr. Thomas woke up, yawned, flicked off the TV and went upstairs to bed. Peace at last.

But the quiet only lasted about ten minutes. Soon Mom brought Beau downstairs and gave him a bottle while she watched TV. When Beau finally fell asleep, Mrs. Thomas yawned and flicked off the TV. Blessed relief.

Five minutes later, Mr. Thomas returned. "Sorry, hamster. Can't sleep," he mumbled to me as he flicked on the remote. He watched and watched and then dozed off again. But the TV stayed on, leaving me no choice but to watch a string of commercials for car waxes, weight-reducing programs, exercise machines and "Red-Hot Harmonica Classics."

The combination of being nocturnal and being bombarded with sight and sound kept me wide-awake.

At the crack of dawn, DeeLee tiptoed into the room, dragging her doll by its hair, and switched to a cartoon show about princesses.

She watched another show about cats and dogs. (Scary!) Then Mr. Thomas woke up and wanted to check some sports scores. Mrs. Thomas handed him the baby and his bottle and soon the older boys switched over to video games and their parents watched them play.

It was LOUD-LOUD-LOUD. But the Thomases didn't seem to notice.

"What do you want for breakfast?" Mom shouted.

"What?" Dad shouted louder.

"WHAT DO YOU WANT FOR BREAKFAST?" Mom yelled.

"TOASTER WAFFLES!" Dad yelled louder.

"I CAN'T HEAR THE TV!" Ty hollered, turning up the volume.

"DO YOU WANT JUICE?" Mom screamed.

"CAN'T HEAR YOU!" Dad responded.

And so it went. With each new question, the sound on the TV would be turned up higher and higher until it was positively deafening.

Then Mom switched on her radio.

The Thomases were a perfectly nice family, but I could tell it was going to be a very long and noisy weekend unless I came up with a Plan.

So, I spun on my wheel for a while to help me think. And I thought and thought and thought some more. And then it came: the Big Idea. I probably would have come up with it sooner if I could have heard myself think!

Around noon, the Thomases were all watching the football game on TV. Or rather, Mr. Thomas was watching the football game on TV while A.J. and Ty shouted questions at him. Mrs. Thomas was in the kitchen listening to the radio and talking on the phone. DeeLee played peekaboo with the baby in the cozy chair.

No one was watching me, so I carefully opened the lock-that-doesn't-lock on my cage and made a quick exit.

Naturally, no one could hear me skittering across the floor as I made my way around the outside of the room, over to the space behind the TV cabinet. Then, with Great Effort, I managed to pull out the plug: one of the most difficult feats of my life.

The TV went silent. Beautifully, blissfully, silently silent. So silent, I was afraid to move. I waited behind the cabinet, frozen.

The Thomases stared at the TV screen as the picture slowly went dark.

"Ty, did you hit that remote?" Mr. Thomas asked.

"Naw. It's under the table."

"Anthony, go turn that thing on again," Mr. Thomas said. A.J. jumped up and hit the power button on the TV.

Nothing happened.

"It's broken!" he exclaimed.

Mrs. Thomas rushed in from the kitchen. "What happened?"

Mr. Thomas explained that the TV had gone off and they discussed how old it was (five years), whether it had a guarantee (no one knew) and if Mr. Thomas could fix it (he couldn't).

"Everything was fine and it went off—just like that.

I guess we'd better take it in to get fixed," Mr. Thomas said.

"How long will it take?" DeeLee asked in a whiny voice.

"I don't know," her dad replied.

"How much will it cost?" Mrs. Thomas asked.

"Oh. Yeah," her husband said. "I forgot. We're a little low on funds right now."

The baby began to cry. I thought the rest of the family might start crying, too.

"Well, I get paid next Friday," Dad said.

A.J. jumped up and waved his hands. "That's a whole week away!"

"I'm going to Grandma's house. Her TV works," said Ty.

"Me, too," DeeLee chimed in.

"Grandma's got her bridge club over there tonight," Mom said.

"I know," said Dad. "Let's go to a movie."

"Do you know how much it costs to go to a movie?" Mom asked. "Besides, we can't take the baby."

"Oh."

They whined and bickered for quite a while. They got so loud, I managed to scamper back to my cage, unnoticed. Then I guess I dozed off. Remember, I had hardly had a wink of sleep since I'd arrived. The bickering was a nice, soothing background after all that racket.

I was only half-asleep when the squabbling changed.

"But there's nothing to do," DeeLee whined.

Her father chuckled. "Nothing to do! Girl, my brothers and I used to spend weekends at my grandma's house and she never had a TV. Wouldn't allow it!"

"What did you do?" A.J. asked.

"Oh, we were busy every minute," he recalled. "We played cards and board games and word games. And we dug in her garden and played tag." He chuckled again. "A lot of times we just sat on the porch and talked. My grandma . . . she could *talk.*"

"What'd you talk about?" Ty wondered.

"Oh, she'd tell us stories about her growing up. About ghosts and funny things, like the time her uncle was walking in his sleep and went to church in his pajamas."

Mrs. Thomas gasped. "Oh, go on now, Charlie."

"I'm just telling you what she told us. He woke up in the middle of the service, looked down and there he was, in his blue-and-white striped pajamas."

I let out a squeak of surprise and the kids all giggled.

Then Mrs. Thomas told a story about a girl in her class who came to school in her slippers by accident one day. "Yes, the fuzzy kind," she explained with a big smile.

They talked and talked and Dad got out some cards and they played a game called Crazy Eights and another one called Pig where they put their fingers on their noses and laughed like hyenas. When Beau fussed, they took turns jiggling him on their knees.

After a while, Mrs. Thomas gasped. "Goodness' sakes! It's an hour past your bedtimes."

The children all groaned and asked if they could play

cards tomorrow and in a few minutes all the Thomases had gone to bed and it was QUIET-QUIET-QUIET for the first time since I'd arrived.

TIP ELEVEN: Be careful. If set free, hamsters are experts at disappearing in a room.

Guide to the Care and Feeding of Hamsters, Dr. Harvey H. Hammer

Peace Breaks Out

Early in the morning, Ty, DeeLee and A.J. raced downstairs and played Crazy Eights. Later, they ran outside and threw a football around the yard.

The Thomases were having breakfast with Beau when the phone rang. Mr. Thomas talked for a few minutes, mostly saying "Uh-huh, that's fine." When he hung up, he told Mrs. Thomas, "We're going to have a visitor. But don't tell Anthony James."

Oooh, a mystery. I like mysteries because they're fun to solve. Then again I don't like mysteries because I don't like not knowing what's going on. So I waited and waited.

A few hours later, the doorbell rang.

The visitor turned out to be Garth Tugwell and his father! "I really appreciate this," Mr. Tugwell told the Thomases. "It was Mrs. Brisbane's idea. Since Garth can't have Humphrey at our house right now, she suggested that he could help A.J. take care of him over here."

Sounds like Mrs. Brisbane. As if I'm trouble to take care of.

But Garth had been crying because he couldn't have me. So maybe—maybe—she was trying to be nice.

After Mr. Tugwell left, Mr. Thomas called A.J. in.

A.J. ran into the room and practically backed out again when he saw Garth.

"We have a guest," said Mr. Thomas. "Shake hands, Anthony. Garth is here to help you take care of Humphrey."

A.J. and Garth reluctantly shook hands.

"How come?" asked A.J.

Garth shrugged his shoulders. "Mrs. Brisbane said to."

"Well, come on. We'll clean his cage and get it over with," A.J. said.

The boys didn't talk much while they cleaned the cage. But they started giggling when they cleaned up my potty corner. (I don't know why that makes everybody giggle.)

After they stopped giggling, they started talking and kidding around. They decided to let me out of the cage, so they took a set of old blocks from DeeLee's room and built me a huge maze. Oh, I love mazes!

When we were all tired of that game, A.J. offered to teach Garth to play Crazy Eights and then Ty and DeeLee joined them in a game of Go Fish.

Nobody mentioned the TV.

Nobody shot any rubber bands.

Later in the afternoon, the kids were all outside playing football. I was fast asleep until Mrs. Thomas came into the den with a broom and started sweeping. A minute later, Mr. Thomas entered.

"What are you doing, hon?"

"What does it look like? I'm sweeping. You know, all the snacking we do in here makes a real mess on the floor," she said.

"Beau's asleep?" her husband asked.

"Uh-huh."

Mr. Thomas walked over to his wife and took the broom away from her. "Then you sit down and rest a spell, hon. I'll sweep. Go on, don't argue."

Mrs. Thomas smiled and thanked him and sat down on the couch. Mr. Thomas swept all around the outside of the room.

Even behind the TV. Uh-oh.

When he got there, he stopped sweeping and leaned down.

"Well, I'll be," he muttered.

"What's wrong?" asked Mrs. Thomas.

"The TV is unplugged," he said. "It's unplugged!" He came out from behind the TV, plug in hand and a very puzzled look on his face.

"But it couldn't have just come unplugged while we were sitting there watching. I mean, a plug doesn't just fall out," he said.

"Plug it in. See if it works," his wife told him.

Well, you guessed it. The TV came on as bright and loud as ever.

"I don't get it," Mr. Thomas muttered. "But at least we don't have to pay to get it fixed."

Mrs. Thomas stared at the screen for a few seconds,

then glanced out the window at the kids playing happily outside.

"Charlie, what do you say we keep it unplugged for a couple more days?" she asked. "We just won't tell the kids."

Mr. Thomas grinned. Then he bent down and unplugged the TV. "Couldn't hurt," he said.

He put down the broom and sat on the couch near his wife and the two of them just sat there in the den, giggling like—well, like Stop-Giggling-Gail!

Suddenly, Mr. Thomas looked over at me.

"You don't mind a little peace and quiet, do you, Humphrey?"

"NO-NO-NO!" I squeaked. And I promptly fell asleep.

Things were a lot better when A.J., Garth and I returned to Room 26. No rubber bands flew through the air. Garth didn't trip anybody or make fun of anybody. That meant Gail didn't get in trouble for giggling. Heidi didn't get in trouble for speaking out without raising her hand because she wasn't trying to tell Mrs. Brisbane what Garth had done.

But the best change was Sayeh, who did raise her hand. Every single day.

One day, she raised her hand to volunteer to stay in during recess to clean the chalkboard. Miranda raised her hand, too. Mrs. Brisbane chose them both.

"Girls, I think I can trust you to stay here while I run

this report down to the principal's office," Mrs. Brisbane told them.

Of course she could trust them.

Once the girls were alone, they began to talk.

"I really liked your singing," Miranda told Sayeh.

"Thanks."

"My mom and I are going to a musical version of 'Cinderella' over at the college this weekend," Miranda continued. "We have an extra ticket. Would you like to come with us? My mom will pick you up."

Sayeh quickly turned to face Miranda. "Oh, yes. I have not been to a play before."

Miranda grinned. "Good! I'll have my mom call your mom."

Suddenly, Sayeh's face fell. "Oh, better not. She's so busy. Ummm. Give me your number and I'll have my father call your mother." Sayeh watched Miranda's reaction carefully. So did I.

"Cool."

That was it. Miranda jotted down her number. Sayeh looked greatly relieved.

I knew that Miranda's mother didn't care how well Sayeh's mother spoke English. Maybe now Sayeh would figure that out, too.

Another great thing that happened was that Mrs. Brisbane started reading a book out loud to the class.

Sometimes, I doze right through these sessions. But this time, she picked out a really good book. When she announced that it was about a mouse, Gail giggled.

"What did she say?" Art whispered to Richie.

"Pay-Attention-Art," Mrs. Brisbane said. "It's about a mouse."

Several of the boys groaned.

"Baby stuff," one of them muttered.

"We'll see," Mrs. Brisbane told them. She started to read and, oh, what a tale it was! All about mice no bigger than I am who were great warriors. I was longing to put on some armor myself by the time she stopped reading.

"Continued tomorrow," she announced as she stuck a bookmark in place and closed the book.

Tomorrow! That woman truly has a mean streak. She's proved it again and again. I would have sneaked out of my cage at night to finish the book, but she's so mean, she stuck it in her desk drawer—the one she locks with a key. Grrrr!

The weekend came around quickly, though, and I went home with Richie.

I'm still not quite sure how many people actually live at the Rinaldis' house because there were always so many people coming and going. Aunts, uncles, cousins, grandparents, neighbors. One meal seemed to flow right into the next and Richie's mom was *very generous* with treats. I'll tell you one thing: You could never be lonely or hungry at the Rinaldis' house.

On Sunday afternoon, guess who showed up? Remember Richie's uncle? That's right: Aldo Amato! This time my buddy Aldo was not lonely because he brought along his girlfriend, Maria, to meet the family. She was a very nice lady who wore her long hair piled up high on her head. She was dressed in bright red from head to toe: red earrings, red sweater, red skirt and red shoes. I think red is a very happy color. I think Maria is a very happy person, especially when she's with Aldo.

All the Rinaldis made a big fuss over Maria and praised the bread and cookies she'd brought from the bakery where she worked.

After all the commotion of their arrival died down, I heard Aldo tell Maria, "Now there's someone really important I want you to meet."

And he introduced her to ME-ME-ME!

"Believe it or not, Humphrey is one of my best friends," he told her. "And he was the very first friend I told about you."

"Then I am honored to meet you, Humphrey," Maria said, smiling down at me.

"The pleasure is all mine!" I squeaked.

"See? He likes you," said Aldo.

And indeed, I did.

❧

The world seemed like a pretty nice place for a handsome young hamster like me, I can tell you. I was sitting on top of the world when I returned to Room 26 on Monday. But I just about toppled off when Mrs. Brisbane made an alarming announcement.

"Class, as you know, this will be a short week, due to Thanksgiving," she said. "And that means Humphrey will need a home for four days instead of two. Now, who wants to volunteer?"

You won't believe what I'm going to say. NOT ONE HAND WENT UP. I actually fell off my wheel.

Mrs. Brisbane was surprised, too. "No one?" she asked. "Heidi, didn't you want to take Humphrey home?"

"Oh, yes. But we're going to my grandma's house for Thanksgiving," she explained.

"Art, didn't you ask for Humphrey last week?" Mrs. Brisbane asked.

"Yes, but we're having all my relatives for Thanksgiving and Mom says it wouldn't be a good time," Art explained.

And so it went. Every single classmate had big plans for Thanksgiving. Plans that didn't include having an extra hamster around.

I was WORRIED-WORRIED-WORRIED. I didn't want to spend four days alone in Room 26.

I worried all day Monday. I worried all day Tuesday. I worried even more all day Wednesday.

At the end of the day, Principal Morales stopped by to give Mrs. Brisbane an envelope. I think it was her paycheck, because she was especially glad to see him.

"I have a huge favor to ask," she said.

"Sure, Sue. What is it?" asked Principal Morales. He wore a tie with little turkeys all over it.

"Could you possibly take Humphrey for the weekend?"

I had my paws crossed that he'd say yes. But Principal Morales didn't even smile.

"Oh, Sue, I'd love to, but we're going out of town for the holiday," he told her. "Another time, I'd love to."

Another time wouldn't matter. I needed a place to go now.

After the principal left, Mrs. Brisbane sighed and began gathering up her papers.

Then she turned to me.

"Well, Humphrey, it looks like you're going home with me for Thanksgiving," she said grimly.

My fate was sealed. I was going to the home of the woman who had once vowed to get rid of me—for four whole days! And frankly, I was worried I'd never come back!

TIP TWELVE: If you must leave your hamster with a caretaker, make sure that it is someone you know and trust.

Guide to the Care and Feeding of Hamsters, Dr. Harvey H. Hammer

Thanks but No Thanks

~•~•~•~•~•~•~•~•~•~

Since Mrs. Brisbane didn't say a word to me on the drive home, I had time to reflect on the last few months. I had not had a bad experience with any of the families I had visited. In fact, they had all been gracious and welcoming (except Miranda's dog, Clem, but I knew how to handle him). In return, I'd lent them a helping paw here and there. After all, you can learn a lot about yourself by getting to know another species.

I was overdue for trouble. And I was likely to get it at Brisbane's House of Horrors. That's how I pictured her home: decorated with skeletons and bats and eerie jack-o'-lanterns all year long. I was shivering at the picture I had in mind when Mrs. Brisbane actually spoke.

"Humphrey, I need you like I need a hole in the head," she complained.

"THE SAME TO YOU!" I squeaked back rudely, knowing she wouldn't understand.

"I don't know what Bert's going to say about you. But whatever it is, it won't be pleasant. Nothing he says is, lately," she continued.

Bert? Who's Bert? Then I realized it must be her husband. The one who's sick. Well, I was certainly not looking forward to meeting him based on what I'd just heard.

"It won't be much of a Thanksgiving," she said. "We don't have much to be thankful for this year. But I'll try."

"Good for you," I squeaked.

She almost smiled. "Thanks for the support."

The Brisbane house was yellow with white shutters and lots of big trees. Colored leaves covered the front yard.

"And on top of everything else, I have to rake!" Mrs. Brisbane said through gritted teeth.

Inside, the house was surprisingly cozy. Not a skeleton or bat in sight. Lots of pretty pictures on the walls and some big yellow flowers in a vase on the table.

"Bert? I'm home," Mrs. Brisbane called out.

A few seconds later, an old man rolled into the room in a wheelchair. His gray hair was uncombed and stuck out in places it shouldn't. His chin was covered with gray stubble and he wore very wrinkled tan pajamas.

His expression was so sour, he looked as if he'd just drunk a glass of vinegar.

Mrs. Brisbane set my cage on the low coffee table.

"We have a guest for the weekend."

I could tell she was trying hard to sound cheery.

"His name is Humphrey."

Mr. Brisbane sneered. "This is unacceptable! For the little pay you get, that school can't force you to spend your weekend baby-sitting a rat!"

I bit my tongue to keep from saying something unsqueakably bad.

"They're not forcing me," argued Mrs. Brisbane. "It's just that no one else could do it. Let's not make a mountain out of a molehill."

Pardon me, but I resented being called a molehill almost as much as being called a rat.

Mrs. Brisbane quickly changed the subject. "I thought you were going to get dressed today."

"Why should I? I'm not going to see anybody," Bert Brisbane growled. "Except you and the rat."

Mrs. Brisbane got up and walked out of the room without saying another word.

Boy, nobody in Room 26 could get away with talking to Mrs. Brisbane like that. I wished I could send her husband to Principal Morales's office right now.

Everything was real quiet around the house for a while. Mrs. Brisbane changed her clothes (to jeans!) and moved my cage onto a card table in the corner of the living room. Then she sat down and read the *Guide to the Care and Feeding of Hamsters* and the chart my classmates kept on me.

"Looks like your friends have been taking good care of you," she said.

"VERY-VERY-VERY GOOD," I squeaked.

She fed me and gave me clean water and then she and Mr. Brisbane ate dinner in some other room while they watched TV. They went to bed early.

I'll bet they didn't say two words to each other. Even

Ms. Mac talked more at home than they did, and she lived alone.

The next morning, Mrs. Brisbane was up very early and soon the house smelled yum-yummy. I thought maybe I would like this Thanksgiving thing after all. At least the good-smelling and eating part.

What I didn't like about Thanksgiving was Mr. Brisbane. While Mrs. Brisbane was clattering pots and clinking pans and making things smell good, he sat in his wheelchair in the living room and frowned. No, I know a better vocabulary word: scowled.

After a while, he called into the kitchen. "Sue, why don't you stop all the cooking and just sit down for a minute?"

Mrs. Brisbane popped her head out the door and said it wouldn't be Thanksgiving without turkey and all the trimmings. Then Mr. Brisbane said he didn't have anything to be thankful for. Mrs. Brisbane went back in the kitchen and banged around some pots and pans again.

That sour expression on the old man's face was starting to get to me, so I decided to take a little spin on my wheel. I really got that thing going at high speed. I was going so fast, I couldn't even see whether Mr. Brisbane was smiling or frowning.

Finally, Mrs. Brisbane came into the room to sit down.

"Would you look at that, Sue?" her husband asked.

"He does that all the time," she said.

"Just spinning his wheels like me. Stuck in a cage and

going nowhere." Mr. Brisbane's voice was so grim, I stopped spinning.

Whew. I was a little dizzy.

"You're wrong, Bert," said Mrs. Brisbane. "Humphrey's not stuck; he goes everywhere. Every weekend, he goes to another house. He eats different foods. He gets out of the cage and runs through mazes. He runs and jumps and climbs. You're the one spinning your wheels and going nowhere. You're stuck in a cage, but it's a cage you made!"

Well. You could have knocked me over with a feather when I heard Mrs. Brisbane talk that way.

Mr. Brisbane was surprised, too.

"Do you think I wanted that car to hit me? Do you think that was my choice?" he asked.

"Of course not, Bert. I'm so grateful you lived through it. That's the point. You're alive, but you sure don't act like it."

With that, Mrs. Brisbane got up and went back into the kitchen. Meanwhile, Mr. Brisbane scowled and frowned and glared . . . at me!

Finally, Mrs. Brisbane put the food on the dining-room table. I watched them eating their dinner from my vantage point on the table in the living room. They ate, but they didn't say much.

"The food is delicious," Mr. Brisbane finally said.

That's the nicest thing I'd heard him say so far.

"Thank you," Mrs. Brisbane replied.

There was silence for a while. Then Mr. Brisbane said, "Just think, last year after Thanksgiving dinner,

Jason and I threw the football around the backyard. Now I'm stuck here and Jason is in Tokyo."

"Let's call him, Bert," his wife suggested.

"It's too early there," he said. "We'll have to call later."

Football. Jason. Tokyo. You can learn a lot if you stop spinning and start listening.

I listened late that night when they called Jason, who turned out to be their grown-up son who was working in Tokyo, which is FAR-FAR-FAR away, even farther than Brazil, according to the maps in Room 26.

Boy, there were more Mrs. Brisbanes than I'd ever dreamed. One was mean to me. One was nice to students. One was a wife. Another one was a mother. One was a cook. One wore dark pantsuits. The other wore jeans.

But which one was the *real* Mrs. Brisbane?

That night, as they headed out of the living room and toward the bedroom, I heard Mrs. Brisbane, the wife, say, "I know you think I was being hard on you, Bert. But it really is time for you to think about what you're going to do with the rest of your life."

Mr. Brisbane didn't answer.

TIP THIRTEEN: Remember, hamsters are very, very curious.
Guide to the Care and Feeding of Hamsters, Dr. Harvey H. Hammer

Hide-and-Go-Squeak

Apparently, the day after Thanksgiving, humans do two things: eat leftovers from the day before and go shopping.

Mr. Brisbane didn't go shopping, of course. But Mrs. Brisbane left early in the morning, after telling Mr. Brisbane that there were plenty of leftovers for him in the refrigerator.

So there I was: stuck with old sourpuss. And all he did was sit in his wheelchair, looking unhappy.

I'd much rather have been hanging out with Principal Morales or chatting with Sayeh's family. I could have been tricking Miranda's dog, playing cards with A.J.'s family or watching Aldo balance a broom on his finger. But no, I was watching a sad and grouchy old man act sad and grouchy.

I could have just settled in for my nap, but I remembered what Mrs. Brisbane had said. This man had to get out of his cage. "Out of your cage!" I squeaked out loud without realizing it.

"Quiet, you little rat," Mr. Brisbane growled at me.

Then he wheeled over to the front window and stared out.

Okay. If he wasn't going to get out of his cage, then I'd get out of mine. Because I had a New Plan.

Mr. Brisbane didn't notice me open the lock-that-doesn't-lock. He didn't see me scamper out of the cage, across the table and onto the couch. He wasn't aware that I leaped down to the floor. He didn't even think about me until I stood in the middle of the living room and said, "CATCH ME IF YOU CAN!"

I know he only heard me squeaking, but I sure got his attention. He was as surprised as could be to see me there.

"How did you get out? And how am I ever going to get you back in?" He rolled toward me. "Come on, whatever-your-name-is. Let's get back in the cage."

I let him get just close enough to reach me. He bent forward, cupping his hands. But just as he reached out to grab me, I dashed over to the opposite side of the room.

"You little rat," he said. "You can't outsmart me."

He rolled over to the closet and took a baseball cap off a hook. Again, he approached and I let him get almost within arm's reach. This time, he raised the baseball cap and said, "Okay, fella. Let's play ball."

"We'll see about that," I squeaked as I bustled off to the living room.

We quickly established the rules of the contest. 1) I would stay out in the open, in places he could reach in his wheelchair. 2) He would use his cap to capture me.

If he could.

Once he reached the dining room, I rushed into the den.

"Oh. Think you're clever. We'll see who's clever," he challenged.

From the den, I scuttled over to the hallway. By now, Mr. Brisbane's cheeks were pink and he was almost smiling.

"You're smart, but you won't win this one!"

This time, I let him get that cap within a whisker of capturing me, just to keep the game interesting. Then I scurried back to the living room. But before he followed me, Mr. Brisbane slammed the bathroom, bedroom and guest-room doors. Aha! He was limiting my range of possibilities. Pretty cunning.

In the living room, I decided to make a bold move. I hid under the couch. Then I let Mr. Brisbane stew for five minutes.

"Come here, Humphrey. You'll have to come out sooner or later," he called. And I thought he didn't know my name.

He shook the curtains and pushed the chairs to see if he could rouse me.

Too bad he didn't think of using sunflower seeds like Mr. Morales did. Yum!

I finally got kind of bored, so I made a dash for the dining room. Mr. Brisbane followed and this time I let him scoop me up in the cap.

"I win!" he shouted triumphantly. He was beaming with pride as he stared down at me. "But you were a worthy opponent."

He put me back in my cage and I scrambled into my sleeping house. I have to admit, the game had made me a little drowsy.

I don't think it was very long before Mrs. Brisbane returned, carrying several shopping bags full of packages.

"What happened, Bert?" she asked when she saw her husband.

"Nothing," he said.

"But your face is all rosy. You look different. And you're wearing a baseball cap," she said.

"Sit down, Sue," he answered. "I'll tell you all about it."

He told her every detail of our match, chuckling and swinging his cap back and forth.

"I guess there are some things I can still do," he said. "Now, how about a game of gin rummy?"

Mrs. Brisbane was almost speechless. "Okay," she said, starting to get up.

Mr. Brisbane waved her away with his cap. "I'll get the cards. You just sit."

As he wheeled into the den, Mrs. Brisbane turned to me and quietly said, "Thank you, Humphrey."

Mr. Brisbane didn't frown the rest of the day and evening, except when Mrs. Brisbane beat him at cards.

The next morning, which was Saturday, she couldn't even find her husband.

"Where could he be?" she asked me. "He hasn't left the house in months!"

A minute later, he came into the house from the garage, his lap full of boards and bricks and things.

"I've got an idea for our friend Humphrey," he said.

Mr. and Mrs. Brisbane spent most of the rest of the day building an obstacle course on the coffee table in the den. They lined up boards along the side (so I couldn't stray too far) and then they set up things for me to climb over and climb under, like bricks with holes to hide in and big cardboard tubes, and Mr. Brisbane constructed a series of ramps for me to climb. Oh, we had a wonderful day. Mr. Brisbane got out a stopwatch to time me on my runs and they made bets on how long it would take me to get from start to finish. Mrs. Brisbane even added a few treats to the maze: bits of apple and biscuit. I had FUN-FUN-FUN. The Brisbanes did, too. I could tell.

On Sunday afternoon, the Brisbanes invited their neighbors over to watch me run my maze. Mr. and Mrs. Robinson brought their five-year-old twins along.

"Glad to see you looking so chipper," Mr. Robinson told Mr. Brisbane.

"I think he's finally feeling better," Mrs. Brisbane whispered to Mrs. Robinson.

Mr. Brisbane looked a little vinegary again on Monday morning, though. "Why can't we keep him here, Sue?" he asked.

"The children would never forgive me," she told him. "He's really their hamster. But . . ." She grinned. "There's a two-week Christmas vacation coming up soon. I think Humphrey better spend it here."

Could I believe my cute, furry ears? She liked me so

much, she actually wanted me to come back! This was a whole new Mrs. Brisbane. One who liked me.

By the time Mrs. Brisbane and I returned to Room 26, I was pretty tired. But it was a good tired and I knew I could rest up from my weekend during recess.

TIP FOURTEEN: Hamsters should be let out of their cages to run in a closed environment for an hour or two at a time.

Guide to the Care and Feeding of Hamsters, Dr. Harvey H. Hammer

Happy Hamsterday

In December, things in Room 26 really began to change. For one thing, it got cold outside and a little chilly by my window. In the early morning, frost pictures would appear on the glass. One picture looked like a big snowflake. Another looked like a lion. Scary.

Still, it was nice and cozy in my sleeping house.

More snowflakes appeared. Not real ones, but cutout paper snowflakes, bordering all the chalkboards. And there were snowmen made of fluffy cotton and pictures of candles and packages and sleighs.

The holidays were almost here: Christmas and Chanukah and Kwanzaa! There were songs to be sung and presents to be wrapped and a big two-week vacation to come!

The weekend after Thanksgiving break, I went home with Pay-Attention-Art. He paid a lot of attention to me.

But sometimes—not every night—during the week, Mrs. Brisbane would take me home to see Mr. Brisbane and he'd put up his obstacle course and we'd laugh and squeak and have a wonderful time.

The next weekend I stayed at Gail Morgenstern's house. Friday night was really nice because she convinced her mom to let me watch while she lit the menorah for the family. And the food was yummy.

I was glad that Mrs. Brisbane didn't take me home every night. For one thing, if I ran the obstacle course every night, I'd probably waste away to nothing. For another thing, I wouldn't have been able to see Aldo.

Aldo could now balance the broom on his head. Yep, he'd put the tip of the broomstick on top of his head and keep it up there a while. He'd have to bob and weave to keep it balanced and he made funny faces, too.

But one night during the week, Aldo pulled his chair up close to my cage and said, "Humphrey, old pal, I've got something to discuss."

This sounded serious, so I put on my most serious, problem-solving face.

"I'm thinking of getting Maria a ring for Christmas. You know, like an engagement ring. With something shiny in it. I know, we haven't known each other very long. And we wouldn't have to get married right away. On the other hand, I'm no spring chicken and I'd like to settle down and raise a couple of kids and maybe a couple of hamsters, too, you know?"

"I understand," I squeaked softly.

"So what do you think?" Aldo fixed his big brown eyes on me. "Should I ask her to marry me?"

I stood up on my hind legs and screeched, "DO IT-DO IT-DO IT!"

Then he stood up and shouted, "You're right! I will! I'd be crazy not to!"

He raced out of the room so fast, he forgot his cleaning cart, but when he returned for it, he yelled, "Thanks!"

Sometimes—most times—it pays to squeak up.

The third weekend after Thanksgiving I spent at Heidi Hopper's house and watched her family put up their Christmas tree. It was the most beautiful thing I'd ever seen, second only to the little tree Heidi put in my cage. It was made of my favorite treat: broccoli!

And then, it was almost holiday vacation.

Suddenly, it seemed as if we didn't have quite as much work to do in class. Everybody was planning the holiday party for the last day of school.

One day, Garth (who never used to wait for the bell) stayed after school to ask Mrs. Brisbane a question.

"May I please bring Humphrey home with me over the holidays?" he asked.

Mrs. Brisbane looked as surprised as I was. "Well, Garth, I thought that was a problem."

Garth smiled broadly. "My mom is much better now and Dad says it's okay to bring Humphrey home."

Mrs. Brisbane smiled back. "That is wonderful news. But I think two weeks might be a little much. How about the first weekend in January?"

Garth nodded, but he looked disappointed.

"Tell you what, why don't you have your parents bring you by our house to see Humphrey over the holidays? You can watch him run his obstacle course."

Garth didn't look disappointed anymore.

On the last day of school, everybody was very dressed up. I had on my fur coat as usual. Mrs. Brisbane wore a red-and-green striped sweater and a green skirt. She also wore a Santa Claus hat.

This was an entirely new Mrs. Brisbane. The dressing-up Mrs. Brisbane.

"Class, I have an important announcement. We're having a surprise visitor this morning, before our party. So there'll be no vocabulary test today."

After the cheers died down, Mrs. Brisbane went out in the hall and waved. A minute later, you'll never guess who entered the classroom. Mr. Bert Brisbane!

He was wearing a Santa Claus hat, too. He looked a lot better now. No gray stubble or wrinkled pajamas. On his lap, he had a large box. Mrs. Brisbane introduced him to the class and they all applauded. Then he told them that his surprise was actually for ME-ME-ME!

First, he pulled out something like my cage—only bigger.

"This is my gift to Humphrey. This extension attaches to his cage and makes it bigger. Now you're all going to help me build Humphrey his holiday present: his very own playground."

The kids squealed and giggled and clapped, and I couldn't hold back a big squeal of my own. I could keep my homey cage with its lock-that-doesn't-lock, but I'd also have my own park to play in!

Mr. Brisbane gathered my classmates around the big table and explained his plans. Mrs. Brisbane unloaded the pieces. First there was a seesaw, then a tree branch to swing from, a big jungle gym and two ladders: one to climb and one to walk across like a bridge. MY-MY-MY!

Sayeh held me while the other kids worked on my cage. She patted me gently and murmured comforting words. Meanwhile, Mr. Brisbane patiently instructed the children as they arranged the pieces. He even made sure everyone got a turn.

Then Mr. Morales dropped by to see how things were going. He was wearing a tie that had little Christmas lights that really lit up!

He and Mrs. Brisbane stood behind the children, watching as my playground took shape.

"Looks like Bert should be a teacher, too," the principal told Mrs. Brisbane.

"He already is," I heard Mrs. Brisbane respond. "He just started teaching arts and crafts to seniors and kids at the Community Center."

"So he's made a new start," said the principal.

"Thanks to Humphrey."

I believe those words were the best present I could ever have.

"Guess what I got my kids for Christmas?" the principal asked. "A hamster. Maybe it's a present for me, as well. I think my papa will enjoy it, too."

When Sayeh put me back in my cage, everyone watched as I raced to my new playground, climbed the jungle gym, made a leap to the tree branch and jumped over to the seesaw. Now I could have recess anytime I wanted. Whoopee!

Just then, the room mothers arrived with cupcakes and juice. While they passed the food out, Sayeh and Miranda slipped quietly out of the room.

A little while later, Mrs. Brisbane announced that she had another surprise: gifts for the class. The door opened and in came Miranda and Sayeh, wearing red dresses trimmed in white fur (not real fur like mine) and white fur hats. They each had a basket filled with small presents and they danced around the room singing a song about the wonders of winter while they passed the gifts out. When the kids opened their packages, they each found a key chain with a small furry toy hamster attached. The hamsters came in all colors: red, green, purple, gold, silver. Nice.

The room mothers presented Mrs. Brisbane with a gift—a pair of red earrings, which she put on right away.

I already thought it was a perfect day. But it wasn't really quite perfect until Mr. Morales peeked out into the hall and announced that *he* had a big surprise.

I wasn't sure we could stand many more surprises.

And then she walked in. The biggest surprise I could imagine.

Ms. Mac was back!

She was wearing a long flowered skirt and a bright red blouse, and she had a butterfly in her hair. (Not a real one, of course.) She also had a huge canvas bag with her.

"Remember me?" she asked with a huge smile.

My classmates were thrilled and they all rushed to her side.

I was so surprised, I was positively squeakless.

119

Mrs. Brisbane made everyone sit down again and asked Ms. Mac (of course, she insisted on calling her Ms. McNamara) about her travels.

Ms. Mac told us about the rain forest and teaching in a school in Brazil. Then she opened her big bag and took out a stack of holiday cards. Her Brazilian students had made a card for each child in Room 26!

While my classmates were sharing their cards with one another, Ms. Mac came over to see me at last.

"Well, I can see by your cage that you've done very well for yourself," she said with a smile. "And here I thought you'd be pining away for me."

"I HAVE!" I squeaked.

She reached into her big bag. "And I have a present for you. But don't tell anybody."

She pulled out a brand-new tiny notebook with blank pages—lots of them. And a new tiny pencil with a very sharp point. "I thought you might need this." Then she tucked it behind my mirror.

Ms. Mac stared at me a little longer, then softly said, "I've seen a lot of creatures in a lot of places in the last few months, but you're still the handsomest and smartest of all."

YES-YES-YES!

"And don't worry. I'll be back to see you again."

She was still the same wonderful Ms. Mac. I'd follow her to the ends of the earth, I thought. Or at least to Brazil.

But then, it hit me. As much as I love her and she loves me, Ms. Mac doesn't need me. Not as much as the

Brisbanes and my classmates and their families do. Maybe that's what Ms. Mac was thinking when she left me in Room 26. This is where I belong.

All too soon, the bell rang. School was over for the day. School was over for the rest of the year. My head was reeling from all the surprises and excitement as we headed out to the car.

In the parking lot, Aldo raced over to greet us and wish us happy holidays. He had come to pick Richie up.

"I hope you have a very happy holiday, too," Mrs. Brisbane told Aldo.

Aldo grinned until his huge mustache shook like Santa's tummy. "I'm sure I will. You see, I just got engaged! I'm going to get married!"

"Yahoo!" I squeaked with delight.

Aldo leaned toward me. "Thanks, my friend."

That night at the Brisbanes' house there was one more surprise. The doorbell rang and a very tall and good-looking young man appeared. He was wearing a Santa Claus hat, but he wasn't Santa.

He was Jason, the Brisbanes' son. He'd come all the way from Tokyo to surprise his parents. They were so happy to see him, they both cried just a little.

I almost cried, too.

Soon, the house was filled with friends and neighbors and Mrs. Brisbane played piano while everyone sang carols and drank hot cider.

I nibbled on raw apple and squeaked along.

Later that night, when the house was quiet, I thought about all I'd done in the months since I had left Pet-O-Rama. I didn't know anything about the world then, but I've sure learned a lot. I can read and write and I know all the state capitals. Just ask me one!

I learned you should never ever turn your back on a dog. And that it's a good idea to turn off the TV once in a while.

I found out kids have problems and so do teachers and principals. Sometimes all people need is a little encouragement.

Most of all, I learned that one small hamster really can make a big difference.

I decided to write down some of the things I've learned from my adventures, but there was just one more line left in my first notebook. So I thought and thought and then I scribbled down exactly what I was feeling deep in my hamster heart:

JOY-JOY-JOY to the WHOLE WIDE WORLD!
(And that includes YOU!)

Humphrey

Humphrey's Guide
to the
Care and Feeding of Humans

1. Like hamsters, humans come in many, many sizes, shapes, colors, talents and tempers. If you judge them by looks alone, you'll miss out on knowing some wonderful people.

2. Humans like to be entertained. And it doesn't take much to entertain them. Just squeak or swing or spin. They'll love it!

3. Humans are pretty entertaining themselves. They can sing, dance, tell jokes and balance brooms.

4. All humans REALLY-REALLY-REALLY need someone to listen to their problems. Preferably someone small and furry.

5. Even really *important* humans (like principals) have problems and need help.

6. Rubber bands hurt. Do *not* shoot rubber bands at one another. *Unless* it's absolutely the only weapon you have against a creature much bigger than you.

7. Humans are not very good at figuring out technical things, like how to fix a broken lock.

8. Humans have unlimited access to all kinds of yummy foods, so be nice to them!

9. If you are nice to humans, they will be nice to you. So nice, they might even build you a playground.

10. Humans have good memories. Even if they go far away to teach in another country, they will not forget you. And believe me, you won't forget them, either!

Most importantly, remember:
You can learn a lot about yourself
by getting to know another species.
Even humans.